F. Ahn

A New, Practical and Easy Method of Learning the German Language

SALZWASSER
VERLAG

F. Ahn

A New, Practical and Easy Method of Learning the German Language

Reprint of the original, first published in 1859.

1st Edition 2022 | ISBN: 978-3-37512-338-3

Verlag (Publisher): Salzwasser Verlag GmbH, Zeilweg 44, 60439 Frankfurt, Deutschland
Vertretungsberechtigt (Authorized to represent): E. Roepke, Zeilweg 44, 60439 Frankfurt, Deutschland
Druck (Print): Books on Demand GmbH, In de Tarpen 42, 22848 Norderstedt, Deutschland

A

N E W,

PRACTICAL AND EASY METHOD

OF

L E A R N I N G

THE GERMAN LANGUAGE.

BY

F. AHN,

Doctor of Philosophy at the College of Neuss.

WITH A PRONUNCIATION, ARRANGED ACCORDING TO

J. C. OEHLSCHLÄGER'S

RECENTLY PUBLISHED

PRONOUNCING GERMAN DICTIONARY.

•

FIRST COURSE.

ELEVENTH EDITION.

PHILADELPHIA:

PUBLISHED BY JOHN WEIK & Co.

1 8 5 9.

a b c d e f g h i j k l m n o p q r

ſ ſs s ß st t u v w x y z

A B C D E F G H I J K L M

N O P Q R S T U V W X Y Z

Der wohlthätigste Besuch, den ein Mensch machen kann, ist der,
wenn er zu sich selbst kommt, denn da lernt er Jemand kennen,
von dem sein ganzes höheres Glück abhängt.
Reden bringt dir Ehre, und Reden bringt dir Schande; Rede

PREFACE TO THE SECOND EDITION.

A few months only have elapsed since we had the pleasure of introducing to the public the first edition of this little work; considering the number of publications of this kind, which the American press has sent forth of late, the undertaking seemed of doubtful success; a discriminating public has however fully sustained the extraordinary reputation, which this text-book of the German language has for some time enjoyed in Europe. Our first edition, which was not inconsiderable, has already disappeared from our shelves, and we have now the pleasure of presenting to our friends a second, revised edition, which, we do not doubt, will be received with equal favor.

Professor Oehlschlæger's system of pronunciation, which we have adapted to this work, has, as we learn from all parts, contributed not a little to facilitate its general introduction. Very few can afford to spend time and money on expensive lessons, and whatever may be said as to the impossibility of describing the sounds of one language by the letters of another, we, as well as many of our friends, have become convinced, since the publication of Oehlschlæger's Pronouncing English and German Dictionaries, together with the present little work, that these do not only facilitate the acquiring of a language with a teacher, but that even without one, a very good pronunciation may be obtained.

Encouraged by numerous applications, and fully convinced of the utility of similar works, we have induced Professor Oehlschlæger to apply his comparative system of pronunciation to the English and French languages, and shall soon be able to lay before the public the result of his labors in a work similar to the present.

THE PUBLISHERS.

I. ALPHABET.

Thᴇ German Alphabet is composed of the following 26 letters:

𝔄,	a,	âh,	a.	𝔑,	n,	en,	n.
𝔅,	b,	bey,	b.	𝔒,	o,	o,	o.
ℭ,	c,	tsey,	c.	𝔓,	p,	pey,	p.
𝔇,	d,	dey,	d.	𝔔,	q,	koo,	q.
𝔈,	e,	ey,	e.	𝔑,	r,	err,	r.
𝔉,	f,	ef,	f.	𝔖,	ſ, ß,	ess,	s.
𝔊,	g,	ghey,	g.	𝔗,	t,	tey,	t.
𝔥,	h,	hâh,	h.	𝔘,	u,	oo,	u.
ℑ,	i,	e,	i.	𝔅,	v,	fou,	v.
ℑ,	j,	yot,	j.	𝔚,	w,	vey,	w.
𝔎,	k,	kâh,	k.	𝔛,	x,	icks,	x.
𝔏,	l,	el,	l.	𝔜,	y,	ip′-see-lon,	y.
𝔐,	m,	em,	m.	𝔷,	z,	tset,	z.

II. PRONUNCIATION OF THE LETTERS.

1. *Simple Vowels.*

𝔄, a, is pronounced like *a* in the English word *father.*

Alter, âl′-ter;   banken, dânk′-en;   Frage, frâ′-gai;
Vater, fâ′-ter;   laben, lâ′-ben;   Galle, gâl′-lai.

Ae, or 𝔄, ä, is the softened vowel 𝔄, a, and is pronounced like *ai* in *fair* or *e* in *met.*

Kälte, kel′-tai,   Käse, kai′-zai;   Blätter, blet′-ter.

ℭ, e, is pronounced like *e* in *let,* or *ai* in *aim,* or *en* in *hen.*

Esel, ai′-zel;   Ende, en′-dai;   trennen, tren′-nen.

ℑ, i, is pronounced like *i* in *is, it, in,* or like *ee* in *bee.*

Lina, lee′-nâ;   finben, fin′-den;   Silber, zil′-ber.

𝔒, o, is pronounced like *o* in the words *no, hope, of.*

Kost, kost;   Ofen, o′-fen;   Rolle, rol′-lai.

Oe, 𝔒, ö, is the softened vowel o. It has no parallel sound in English; the *i* in *bird* and the *e* in *her* sound very nearly like it.

Löwe, lö′-vai;   böse, bö′-zai;   Löffel, löf′-fel.

𝔘, u, is pronounced like *oo* in *root,* or like *u* in *put.*

(The pronunciation of the short *u* is marked thus: "ŏŏ"; of the long *u* thus "oo".)

Blume, bloo′-mai;   Mutter, mŏŏt′-ter;   Munb, mŏŏnt.

Ue, 𝔘, ü, is the softened vowel u, and has no parallel sound in English. It is pronounced like *u* in French.

Übel, ü′-bel;   mübe, mü′-dai;   Nüsse, nüss′-sai.

𝔜, y, has the sound of the German i, which is now generally employed in its stead.

(5)

2. Double Vowels.

The double vowels aa, ee, oo are no diphthongs, because only one letter is sounded, and the second only serves to indicate that the syllable is long.

Aar, åhr; Seele, zey'-lai; Boot, bote.

Je, ie, is pronounced like ee in *meet*.

Biene, bee'-nai; tief, teef; lieben, lee'-ben.

3. Diphthongs.

In the German diphthongs, the two vowels must be sounded one after the other, but so quickly as to form only one syllable.

Ai and ei are pronounced almost alike, and have the sound of the English *i* in the word *fire.*'

Saite, zi'-tai; Seite, zi'-tai; reimen, ri'-men.

Au is pronounced like *ou* in *house.*

Maus, mouse; Baum, boum; blau, blou.

Äu and eu are both pronounced like *oi* in *oil*, or *oy* in *boy.*

Mäuse, moi'-zai; Beutel, boi'-tel; Freund, froint.

4. Consonants.

At the beginning of syllables, these differ but little from the English, as the end b has the sound of p, b of t, g of ch or k, v of f and s of ß.

C, c, before ä, e and i is pronounced like *ts.*

Cäsar, tsai'-zår; Ceder, tsai'-der; Citrone, tsee-tro'-nai.

Before a, o, u, before a consonant and at the end of a syllable it is pronounced like *k*, by which in most cases it may be replaced.

Carl, Kårrl; Conrad, Kon'-råht; Tombac, tom'-båck.

Ch, at the beginning of a word is pronounced like k, except in words derived from the French, when it preserves the French pronunciation.

Chor, kore; Christ, krist; Charlatan, shår'-lå-tån.

In the middle or at the end of a word ch has a pronunciation peculiar to the German language, and more or less guttural, and for which no corresponding sound can be found in English; it is like the Scotch *ch* in the word *loch* after a, o, u, au, but softer after ä, e, i, ö, ü, äu, eu, and after a consonant.

Dach, dåch; Rauch, rouch; nichts, nichts;

Loch, loch; Küche, küch'-chai; rechnen, rech'-nen;

Buch, booch; Tochter, toch'-ter; Bäumchen, boim'-chen.

chs or chf is pronounced like *cks* when these consonants belong to the root or radical syllable.

Wachs, våcks; Fuchs, foocks; Ochs, ocks.

But the ch preserves its guttural pronunciation, when it stands before the s or f by contraction or in a compound word.

nachsehen, nach''-zey-hen; des Buchs, boochs, instead of des Buches, boo'-chess.

G, g, at the beginning of a syllable it is pronounced hard, like the English *g* in the word *good.*

Gabe, gå'-bai gehen, ghey'-hen; Gruß, grooss;

At the end of a syllable, except after **u**, it has the sound of **ᾐ**, only much softened and with this difference, that the g generally leaves the preceding vowel long whilst the **ᾐ** shortens it.

    Sieg, *zeeᾐ*;   artig, ähr'-tiᾐ;   Tag, tähᾐ.

After **n** at the end of a word it is pronounced like soft **k**.

    Gang, gânk;   Sprung, spröönk;   Hang, hânk.

H, h, is always aspirated at the beginning of a syllable.

    hier, here;   hart, hârrt;   Hecht, hecht;
    Haus, house;   Himmel, him'-mel;   Freiheit, fri'-hite.

The aspiration becomes however almost imperceptible before an **e** in the end syllables.

    Reihe, ri'-(h)ai;   Ruhe, roo'-(h)ai;   sehen, zey'-(h)en.

After a vowel or a **t**, the **h** is not pronounced; but, only indicates that the syllable is long.

    Hahn, hähn;   Mehl, mail;   Uhr, oor.
    Reh, rey;   Rath, râht;   Thier, teer.

J, j, only stands at the beginning of a syllable, and is pronounced like the English y in the word *yet*.

    Jahr, yähr;   Joch, yoch;   Jugend, yoo'-ghent.

ck replaces the double **k**, and is pronounced short.

    Stock, stook;   Brücke, brück'-kai;   Acker, âck'-ker.

S, f, s, at the beginning of a syllable is pronounced like the English **z**; at the end of a syllable, however, like the English **s**.

    Sommer, zom'-mer;   Reise, ri'-zai;   Haus, house;
    Sack, zâck;   Eisen, i'-zen;   Reis, rice.

The long **f** is placed at the beginning and in the middle, **s** only at the end of syllables. If in a non-compound word there are two **f** one after another, they are written **ff**.

    Wasser, vâss'-ser;   wissen, viss'-sen;   müssen, müss'-sen.

ß is only placed at the end or in the middle of syllables; it is always preceded by a long vowel, and has the sound of the English sharp **s** or **ss**.

    Straße, strâ'-sai;   groß, gro'ss;   fließen, flee'-sen.

Sch, sch, is pronounced like the English **sh**.

    Schatten, shât'-ten;   Schule, shoo'-lai;   Peitsche, pite'-shai;
    schlafen, shlâ'-fen;   Schild, shilt;   Tisch, tish.

st and **sp** are pronounced like *st* and *sp* in English.

    Stuhl, stool;   stehlen, stai'-len;   spielen, spee'-len,
    Stern, sterrn;   sprechen, sprech'-chen;   stechen, stech'-chen.

V, v, has the sound of *f*.

    Vater, fâ'-ter;   Vogel, fo'-ghel;   Vieh, fee.

W, w, is pronounced like the English **v**.

    Welt, velt;   Wiese, vee'-zai;   Wand, vânt.

t

3, ʒ, is sounded like *ts.*

Zaȟl, tsåhl;   Zorn, tsorrn;   Holʒ, hŏlts;

Zeit, tsaite;   ʒwanʒig, tsvån'-tsiȟ;   Herʒ, herrts·

ʒ replaces the double **ʒ** and is pronounced very hard.

Bliʒ, blits;   Ruʒen, nŏŏt'-tsen;   ʃeʒen, zet'-tsen.

III. SYLLABIC ACCENT.

The Accent is on the root of the word.

In verbs beginning with a separable particle, and in words derived from such verbs, this particle has the primary accent.

Words terminating in *ei* or *ey* have the accent on the last syllable.

In compound words, the root of the qualifying word has the primary accent.

IV. DIVISION OF SYLLABLES.

The general rule for division is: "*Divide, as you speak.*"

1) A simple consonant between two vowels is joined to the latter. Except the letter **r**; as, Her-en.

2) Of two consonants, meeting between two vowels, one is joined to the preceding and the other to the following syllable. — ȟ, ſȟ, pȟ, tȟ, ſt, ſp, d, ʒ, ß are treated as simple consonants.

3) When three or four consonants, which are not proper to begin a syllable, meet between two vowels, such of them as can begin a syllable, belong to the latter, the rest to the former syllable; as, Men-ſȟen, bie Deut-ſȟen.

4) A compound word is divided according to its elements.

EXPLANATION
OF THE SIGNS USED IN THE PRONUNCIATION.

å, represents the German a; like all the vowels, it is long at the end of a syllable, short before one or more consonants. To represent the long sound before a consonant å is changed into åh.

ai, ey, the former, when accented, represents the German long and open e, as *ai* in the word *air*, the latter the long and close e, as *ey* in *obey*. When unaccented the former represents the sound of *ey* in the noun *survey*.

oo, ŏŏ, the former is long, as *oo* in *boot*, the latter short, as *oo* in *foot* or *u* in *put*.

ou, always like *ou* in *pound.*

' An apostrophe after the vowel makes it long before a consonant, where in English it would be short, or might be either short or long.

˘ A breve over the vowel, makes it short, where it would be long, or might be either long or short.

′ indicates the accented syllable.

″ Compound words have frequently two accented syllables, the primary accent is indicated by ″, the secondary by ′.

ŏ, ü and ȟ, these have no corresponding sounds or characters in English, and are therefore indicated in the same manner as in German.

In every other respect each syllable must be pronounced as in English.

PART 1.

In the following exercises the English idiom has been frequently sacrificed to facilitate the labors of the student; thus, for the compound tenses of intransitive verbs, the auxiliary "to be" has been substituted for "to have," &c.

1.

Singular.	ich bin, ich bin,	I am;
	du bift, doo bist,	thou art;
	er ift, air ist,	he is;
	fie ift, zee ist,	she is;
	es ift, ess ist,	it is;
Plural.	wir find, veer zint,	we are;
	ihr feid, eer zite,	you are;
	fie find, zee zint,	they are.

Gut, goot, good; groß, gro'ss, large; flein, kline, little, small; reich, ri'ch, rich; arm, ârm, poor; jung, yŏŏnk, young; alt, ält, old; müde, mü'-dai, tired; frank, krânk, sick.

Ich bin groß. Du bift flein. Er ift alt. Sie ift gut. Wir find jung. Ihr feid reich. Sie find arm. Bin ich groß? Bift du müde? Ift er frank? Ift fie jung? Sind wir reich? Seid ihr arm? Sind fie alt?

2.

I am little. Thou art young. We are tired. They are rich. Art thou sick? You are poor. Is she old? Are you sick? Are they good? He is tall (groß). Am I poor?

3.

Nicht, nicht, not.

Start, stârk, strong; treu, troi, faithful; faul, foul, idle, lazy; fleißig, fli'-sich, diligent; böfe, bö'-zai, wicked, naughty; traurig, trou'-rich, sad; glücflich, glück'-lich, happy; höflich, hö'f'-lich, polite.

Bift du böfe? Ich bin nicht böfe. Er ift traurig. Wir find nicht ftark. Sind fie treu? Bift du nicht glücflich? Ihr feid nicht fleißig. Sie ift nicht faul. Ift er nicht müde? Wir find nicht arm. Sind fie nicht höflich? Du bift nicht frank.

4.

I am not tall. They are idle. She is not ill. We are not happy. He is not short (flein). Are you not tired? They are not rich. Is he not diligent? Thou art not strong. They are not happy. He is not polite. Are they not faithful? Is she not rich? He is not wicked.

5.

Masculine nouns: ber Vater, dair fä'-ter, the father.
ber Garten, dair gärr'-ten, the garden.
Feminine — bie Mutter, dee mööt'-ter, the mother.
bie Stabt, dee stät, the town.
Neuter — bas Kinb, dâss kint, the child.
bas Haus, dâss house, the house.

Schön, shö'n, beautiful, fine; lang, lâng, long; hoch, ho'ch, high; neu, noi, new; unb, öönt, and; sehr, zeyr, very.

Der Vater ist gut. Die Mutter ist traurig. Das Kinb ist faul. Der Garten ist nicht sehr lang. Die Stabt ist groß unb reich. Das Haus ist nicht hoch. Ist ber Garten schön? Ist ber Vater krank? Ist bas Kinb nicht fleißig? Ist bas Haus neu? Der Vater unb bie Mutter sinb glücklich.

Observation 1. All German nouns begin with a capital letter.
Obs. 2. When two or more nouns follow each other, the article must be repeated before each, unless they are all of the same gender.

6.

The house is not new. The mother and (the) child are ill. The town is very beautiful. The child is not naughty. The father is very old. The house and (the) garden are very large. Is the mother not happy? The house is not very old. Is the garden not very fine? The house is very small.

7.

Masc. bieser Baum, dee'-zer boum, this tree.
Fem. biese Frau, dee'-zai frou, this woman.
Neut. bieses Pferb, dee'-zes pfairt, this horse.

Der Mann, dair mân, the man; ber Berg, dair berrch, the mountain; bie Blume, dee bloo'-mai, the flower; bas Fenster, dâss fen'-ster, the window; offen, of'-fen, open; zufrieben, tsoo-free'-den, satisfied, contented, pleased; ober, o'-der, or.

Dieser Mann ist sehr arm. Dieses Fenster ist sehr hoch. Diese Blume ist schön. Dieses Pferb ist jung unb stark. Ist biese Frau glücklich? Dieser Vater unb biese Mutter sinb nicht zufrieben. Dieser Baum ist sehr groß. Diese Frau ist arm unb krank. Dieses Kinb ist sehr böse. Dieser Mann ist nicht höflich. Bist bu traurig ober krank?

8.

This woman is tired. This mountain is not high. Is this child good or naughty? This man is not satisfied. This child is not very diligent. Is this garden small or large? Art thou not contented? This window is not open. Is this house old or new? This tree is very fine. Is this man rich or poor? This town is very dull (traurig).

9.

Masc.	*Fem.*	*Neut.*
Ein, ine,	eine, i'-nai,	ein, ine, a;
mein, mine,	meine, mi'-nai,	mein, mine, my;
bein, dine,	beine, di'-nai,	bein, dine, thy.

Der Bruder, dair broo'-der, the brother; die Schwester, dee shwess'-ter, the sister; die Feder, dee fai'-der, the pen; das Buch, dâss. booch, the book; der Freund, dair froint, the friend; Karl, Kârl, Charles: Luise, Loo-ee'-zai, Louisa; wo, vo, where; hier, here, here; noch, noch, still, yet; aber, â'-ber, but; Berlin, berr-leen', Berlin.

Mein Bruder ist traurig. Meine Schwester ist krank. Mein Buch ist schön. Ist dein Garten groß? Ist deine Feder gut? Ist dein Pferd klein? Karl ist noch ein Kind. Berlin ist eine Stadt. Luise ist meine Schwester. Dein Bruder ist mein Freund. Dein Vater ist nicht hier. Wo ist mein Buch? Ist mein Buch nicht hier? Ist deine Mutter noch krank? Ich bin noch nicht müde, aber dein Bruder und deine Schwester sind sehr müde.

10.

Charles is my brother. This child is my sister. Thou art my friend. Thy garden is very large. Where is thy mother? A friend is faithful. Is this child thy brother? This horse is still young. Where is my pen? Thy pen is here. Louisa is still a child. Thy brother is idle. My friend is very diligent.

11.

Masc.	Fem.	Neut.	
Unser, ŏŏn'-zer,	unsere, ŏŏn'-zai-rai,	unser, ŏŏn'-zer,	our;
euer, oi'-er,	euere, oi'-ai-rai,	euer, oi'-er,	your;
ihr, eer,	ihre, ee'rai,	ihr, eer,	their.

Der Sohn, dair zone, the son; die Tochter, dee toch'-ter, the daughter; immer, im'-mer, always.

Obs. In addressing any one, the third person plural is from politeness used instead of the second: **Sie sind**, instead of **ihr seid**. For the same reason **Ihr** is used instead of **euer**. In this case the pronoun is always written with a capital letter.

Unser Garten ist groß. Unsere Mutter ist krank. Unser Pferd ist schön. Dieser Mann ist unser Vater. Diese Frau ist unsere Mutter. Karl ist euer Bruder. Luise ist eure Schwester. Ist Ihr Sohn fleißig? Ist Ihre Tochter zufrieden? Wo ist Ihr Buch? Unser Haus ist alt. Unsere Thür ist immer offen. Dieser Vater und diese Mutter sind sehr traurig; ihr Sohn ist immer krank.

12.

Our father is good. Our mother is little. Our child is ill. Is this man your brother? Is this woman your mother? Your son is not always diligent. Is your horse beautiful? This child is our brother. Is Charles not your friend? Louisa is not your sister.

13.

Klein, kline, little, small;		kleiner, kli'-ner, smaller;		
alt, âlt, old;		älter, el'-ter, older;		
groß, gro'ss, great;		größer, grö'-ser, greater;		
jung, yŏŏnk, young;		jünger, yüng'-er, younger;		
fleißig, fli'-sich, diligent;		fleißiger, fli'-sig-er, more diligent.		

Nützlich, nüts'-lich, useful; unglücklich, öon''-glück'-lich, unhappy, unfortunate; der Hund, dair höönt, the dog; die Katze, dee kât'-tsai, the cat; die Sonne, dee zon'-nai, the sun; der Mond, dair mo'nt, the moon; als, âlss, than, as.

Obs. In forming the Comparative of an adjective, the radical vowel a generally changes into ä, o into ö, and u into ü.

Mein Bruder ist älter, als ich. Ich bin jünger, als mein Freund. Karl ist größer, als Luise. Dieser Mann ist größer, als wir. Der Hund ist treuer, als die Katze. Das Pferd ist schöner und nützlicher, als der Hund. Dieses Kind ist fleißiger, als du. Sie sind glücklicher, als Ihr Bruder. Karl ist stärker, als ich. Wir sind zufriedener, als ihr. Luise ist höflicher, als deine Schwester. Ist dein Bruder jünger, als du? Er ist älter, aber kleiner, als ich.

14.

My brother is more diligent than thou. Thou art not younger than he. He is taller and stronger than I. Your son is younger than this child. The moon is smaller than the sun. Art thou older than I? This dog is finer than this cat? Your sister is politer than you. I am more contented than thou. You are richer than we. We are more unhappy than you.

15.

Gut, goot, good; besser, bess'-ser, better; hoch, ho'ch, high; höher, hö'-her, higher.

Dieser, diese, dieses, dee'-zer, dee'-zai, dee'-zess, this, this one; jener, jene, jenes, yai'-ner, yai'-nai, yai'-ness, that, that one.

Das Eisen, dâss i'-zen, the iron; das Blei, dâss bli, the lead; der Stahl, dair stâhl, the steel; schwer, shwair, heavy; hart, hârt, hard; theuer, toi'-er, dear; so, zo, so, as; zu, tsoo, too; wie, vee, as.

Mein Buch ist schöner, als jenes. Meine Feder ist besser, als diese. Der Stahl ist härter, als das Eisen. Dieser Berg ist höher, als jener. Die Katze ist nicht so treu, wie der Hund. Das Blei ist nicht so hart, wie das Eisen. Ist Ihr Haus nicht größer, als jenes? Ist das Blei theurer, als das Eisen? Der Mond ist nicht so groß, wie die Erde. Dieses Kind ist fleißiger, als jenes. Jene Frau ist ärmer, als diese. Unser Garten ist nicht so lang und schön, wie dieser.

16.

(The) lead is heavier than (the) iron. This tree is not so high as that. Is this book not better than that? Our garden is smaller than this one. This house is higher than that one. (The) iron is more useful than (the) lead. I am not so old as he. (The) lead is not so dear as (the) steel. Our town is larger and finer than this one. We are not so rich as this man, but we are more contented than he.

17.

Singular.	ich habe, ich hâ'-bai,	I have;
	du haft, doo hâst,	thou hast;
	er, sie, es hat, air, zee, ess hât,	he, she or it has;
Plural.	wir haben, veer hâ'-ben,	we have;
	ihr habet, eer hâ'-bet,	you have;
	sie haben, zee hâ'-ben,	they have.

Die Uhr, *tee oor,* the watch; das Messer, *dâss mess'-ser,* the knife; Recht, recht, right; Unrecht, öön'-recht, wrong; Heinrich, Hine'-rich, Henry; Ludwig, Loot'-vich, Lewis; für, fü'r, for.

Obs. 1. The Accusative (Objective Case) of the fem. and neut. nouns is like the Nominative.

Obs. 2. In German the verb *to have* is used with *right* and *wrong,* and not the verb *to be* as in English; thus: Ich habe Recht; not, ich bin Recht.

Ich habe Recht. Du hast Unrecht. Ich habe ein Buch. Du hast eine Feder. Mein Bruder hat eine Uhr. Wir haben ein Haus. Ihr habt ein Pferd. Karl und Luise haben eine Katze. Hast du eine Schwester? Hat dieser Mann eine Tochter? Habt ihr ein Kind? Diese Uhr ist für meine Mutter. Diese Feder ist für Karl. Haben Sie noch Ihre Mutter? Warum hast du mein Messer? Ich habe dein Messer nicht.

18.

Charles, hast thou my pen? Louisa, hast thou my book? Henry has thy pen, and Lewis has thy book. Thou art right. My son is wrong. We have a book and a pen. Have you also a horse and a watch? This knife is for Henry. Is this watch for thy mother? Has your friend a knife? Charles and Lewis have a horse. Has your father still a sister? Is this flower for my daughter?

19.

Gesehen, gai-zey'-hen, seen; verloren, ferr-lo'-ren, lost; gefunden, gai-föön'-den, found; gekauft, gai-kouft', bought; verkauft, ferr-kouft', sold; genommen, gai-nom'-men, taken; warum, vâ'-rööm, why.

Obs. The past participle is detached from the auxiliary and placed at the end of the sentence.

Ich habe mein Buch verloren. Hast du mein Messer gefunden? Ich habe dein Messer nicht gefunden. Wo ist meine Feder? Habt ihr meine Feder? Wir haben deine Feder nicht. Mein Vater hat dieses Pferd gekauft. Wir haben unser Haus verkauft. Wo hast du meine Uhr gefunden? Warum haben Sie meine Uhr genommen? Ich habe Ihre Mutter und Ihre Schwester gesehen. Warum hat Ihr Vater dieses Haus nicht gekauft? Hat dein Bruder meine Feder genommen? Er hat deine Feder nicht genommen.

20.

Where hast thou found this book? Have you lost your pen? Has your father bought this horse? Why have you sold your watch? Why have you not taken my pen? My brother has found thy knife. We have seen thy mother. I have not yet seen this woman. Charles and Lewis have lost their mother; they are very sad.

21.

Nominative.	*Accusative* (Objective case).	
Der Vater, dair fä'-ter,	den Vater, dain fä'-ter,	the father.
dieser Vater, dee'-ser fä'-ter,	diesen Vater, dee'-zen fä'-ter,	this father.

Der König, dair kö'-nich, the king; der Hut, hoot, the hat, bonnet; der Stock, stock, the stick, cane; der Brief, breef, the letter; geschrieben, gai-shree'-ben, written; erhalten, err-hâl'-ten, received, got; oft, oft, often; schon, sho'n already.

Obs. The subject is placed in the nominative case, and the object in the accusative case.

Ich habe den König gesehen. Hast du den Brief erhalten? Meine Schwester hat den Brief nicht geschrieben. Heinrich hat den Stock verloren. Mein Vater hat diesen Garten und dieses Haus gekauft. Wo habt ihr diesen Hund und diese Katze gefunden? Ich habe diesen Mann schon oft gesehen. Warum haben Sie diesen Hut genommen? Wir haben diesen Brief gefunden. Hat dein Bruder diesen Stock verloren?

22.

We have sold the house and garden. Have you bought this dog and this horse? I have seen the man and woman, the son and daughter. I have not written this letter. Where have you found this book and cane? Has thy brother bought this tree? This letter is for this man. Hast thou lost this hat? Hast thou not taken this book and pen? Hast thou already seen the king? I have not yet seen the king.

23.

Nom. ein Garten,		
Accus. einen (i'-nen) Garten,	} a garden.	

Nom. mein Hund,		
Accus. meinen (mi'-nen) Hund,	} my dog.	

Der Vogel, fo'-ghel, the bird; der Stuhl, stool, the chair; der Tisch, tish, the table; der Bleistift, bli'-stift, the pencil; der Nachbar, nâch'-bâhr, the neighbor.

Mein Bruder ist sehr zufrieden; er hat einen Vogel. Hast du einen Brief erhalten? Ich habe meinen Hut verloren. Haben Sie meinen Hund schon gesehen? Wir haben einen Tisch und einen Stuhl gekauft. Mein Bruder hat deinen Stock genommen. Wo hast du deinen Bleistift gekauft? Wir haben unsern Vater und unsere Mutter verloren. Ich habe Ihren Brief nicht erhalten. Hat dein Bruder unsern Garten und unser Haus schon gesehen? Unser Nachbar hat den König gesehen. Hast du diesen Vogel gekauft oder jenen?

24.

We have lost our dog. This man has lost a son and a daughter. Where have you found my pencil? Have you already seen

my brother and mother? I have bought a bonnet for my sister.
Our neighbor has found thy knife and cane. Where hast thou
bought this table? Thy brother has taken my chair. Have you
written a letter? We have found this stick and that one.

25.

Nom. ſein, ſeine, ſein, zine, zi′-nai, zine, } his, its.
Accus. ſeinen, ſeine, ſein, zi′-nen, zi′-nai, zine,

Nom. ihr, ihre, ihr, eer, ee′-rai, eer, } her.
Accus. ihren, ihre, ihr, ee′-ren, ee′-rai, eer,

Geleſen, gai-lai′-zen, read; gekannt, gai-kānt′, known; der Onkel, onk′-el, the
uncle; die Tante, tān′-tai, the aunt; der Fingerhut, fing′-er-hoot, the thimble; die
Scheere, shai′-rai, the scissors.

Mein Freund iſt traurig, ſein Vater und ſeine Mutter ſind krank.
Meine Tante iſt zufrieden; ihr Sohn und ihre Tochter ſind ſehr fleißig.
Heinrich hat ſeinen Stock, ſeine Uhr und ſein Meſſer verloren. Luiſe
hat ihren Fingerhut, ihre Feder und ihr Buch verloren. Euer Onkel
hat ſein Haus und ſeinen Garten verkauft. Dieſe Frau hat ihren Mann
und ihr Kind verloren. Dieſe Tochter hat einen Brief für ihre Mutter
geſchrieben. Karl hat ſeinen Vater nicht gekannt. Die Tante hat deinen
und meinen Brief geleſen.

26.

The father has lost his son. This mother has lost her daughter.
My uncle has sold his watch. Our aunt has sold her scissors.
Henry has found his pencil. Louisa has found her thimble. I have
seen this man and his son, this woman and her daughter. My
mother has lost her pen and her knife. My brother has taken
his hat. I have seen your aunt; has she still her horse? This man
is very sad; he has lost his wife (Frau). Charles has written a
letter for his father. My aunt has bought this book for her son.

27.

Nom. die Mutter, the mother;
Gen. (Possessive Case) der Mutter, the mother's, of the mother;
Nom. dieſe Mutter, this mother;
Gen. dieſer Mutter, this mother's, of this mother.

Die Magd, mähcht, the maid-servant; die Königin, kö′-nig-in, the queen; die
Nachbarin, nāch′-bā-rin, the female neighbor; angekommen, ān″-gai-kom′-men,
arrived; abgereiſt, āp″-gai-ri′st′, departed.

Die Mutter der Königin iſt angekommen. Der Vater der Nachbarin
iſt abgereiſt. Ich habe den Garten der Tante geſehen. Haben Sie den
Bleiſtift der Schweſter gefunden? Dieſe Frau iſt die Schweſter der
Nachbarin. Dieſer Mann iſt der Bruder der Magd. Das Kind dieſer
Frau iſt immer krank.

28.

The bonnet of the mother is beautiful. The sister of the queen is not beautiful. Is the father of the servant arrived? Are you the brother of the (female) neighbor? I am the sister of this woman. Hast thou taken the chair of the sister? Have you seen the horse of the aunt? We have known the father of this servant.

29.

Nom. der Vater, the father;
Gen. des Vaters, dess fä'-ters, of the father;
Nom. das Kind, kint, the child;
Gen. des Kindes, dess kin'-dess, of the child;

dieser Vater', this father;
dieses Vaters, of this father;
dieses Kind, this child;
dieses Kindes, of this child.

Der Schuhmacher, shoo'-mäch-cher, the shoemaker; der Schneider, shni'-der, the tailor; der Gärtner, ghernt'-ner, the gardener; der Kaufmann, kouf'-mân, the merchant; der Arzt, ârtst, the physician; die Thür, tü'r, the door; das Zimmer, tsim'-mer, the room; das Volk, fol'k, the people.

Obs. All neuter nouns and most masculine nouns take s or es in the Genitive Singular.

Die Magd des Schneiders ist krank. Der Sohn des Nachbars ist noch sehr jung. Die Blume des Gärtners ist sehr schön. Der Garten des Königs ist sehr groß. Der König ist der Vater des Volkes. Die Frau des Arztes ist immer zufrieden. Ich habe den Garten des Onkels gesehen. Wir haben das Pferd des Kaufmanns gekauft. Hast du den Bleistift des Bruders genommen? Wo ist die Magd des Schuhmachers? Die Thür des Zimmers ist immer offen. Die Tochter dieses Mannes ist abgereist. Wir haben die Mutter dieses Kindes gekannt. Der Garten dieses Hauses ist klein.

30.

This man is the brother of the gardener. This woman is the sister of the shoemaker. This child is the son of the tailor. The door of the house is not open. I have seen the son and daughter of the physician. We have seen the horse of the merchant. The servant of the neighbor is the sister of this gardener. Why is the door of this room open? We have known the son of this merchant. The dog of the neighbor is faithful. The mother of this child has arrived.

31.

Nom. ein Vater, eine Mutter, ein Kind;
Gen. eines (i'-ness) Vaters, einer (i'-ner) Mutter, eines Kindes.

Der Regenschirm, rai''-ghen-shirrm', the umbrella; das Federmesser, .fai''-der-mess'-ser, the penknife; gestern, gess'-tern, yesterday.

Obs. The pronouns mein, dein, sein, ihr, unser, euer, are declined like ein, eine, ein.

Sind Sie der Sohn eines Arztes? Ich bin der Sohn eines Kaufmanns. Haben Sie das Haus meines Nachbars gekauft? Der Bruder deines Freundes ist gestern angekommen. Wo ist der Regenschirm deiner

Onkels? Haſt du das Zimmer meiner Schweſter geſehen? Wir haben den Brief deiner Mutter geleſen. Mein Onkel hat das Haus Ihres Vaters gekauft. Ich habe den Stock Ihres Bruders verloren. Der Garten unſeres Nachbars iſt ſehr groß. Unſere Magd iſt die Tochter eures Gärtners. Wo iſt der Regenſchirm unſerer Mutter? Karl hat den Fingerhut ſeiner Schweſter genommen. Luiſe hat das Federmeſſer ihrer Tante genommen.

32.

I have found the hat of a child. Are you the servant of my uncle? I am the servant of your tailor. The penknife of thy brother is very good. The pen of thy sister is not good. The house of our aunt is large. Henry has lost the letter of his father. Louisa has found the pen of her brother. Is the garden of our uncle as fine as this one? We have found the hat of your neighbor's son (the hat of the son of your neighbor). Lewis has read the letter of his friend. Louisa has bought a flower for a child of her sister.

33.

Nom. der Bruder,　　the brother;
Dat. dem (daim) Bruder, to the brother.

Nom. das Buch, the book;　　die Schweſter, the sister;
Dat. dem Buche, to the book;　ber Schweſter, to the sister.

Gehört, gai-hör't, belongs; geliehen, gai-lee'-hen, lent; gegeben, gai-gai'-ben, given; geſchickt, gai-shickt', sent; verſprochen, fer-sproch'-chen, promised; gezeigt, gai-tsi'cht, shown; der Freund, froint, the friend; die Freundin, froin'-din, the female friend.

Obs. 1. If the Genitive terminates in es, the Dative takes e, Buches, Buche.
Obs. 2. The Dative is used in answer to the questions, to whom, and to what?—and generally precedes the Accusative.
Obs. 3. In interrogative and negative sentences the English auxiliary verb to do is not translated in German.

Dieſes Haus gehört dem Onkel meines Nachbars. Jener Garten gehört der Tante meines Freundes. Ich habe dem Vater einen Brief geſchrieben. Sie hat der Freundin ihrer Schweſter eine Blume gegeben. Karl hat der Schweſter ſein Federmeſſer geliehen. Haſt du dem Arzte mein Buch geſchickt? Ich habe dieſem Kinde einen Vogel verſprochen. Heinrich hat dieſer Frau unſern Regenſchirm geliehen. Luiſe hat dieſem Manne unſern Garten gezeigt. Ich habe meine Feder dem Freunde meines Bruders gegeben.

34.

The hat belongs to the gardener. This house belongs to the mother of my friend. I have written to my uncle and aunt. My sister has lent her thimble to the friend (fem.) of your brother. My uncle has sent a watch to the son of your neighbor (fem.). Have you given a chair to this child? Have you lent an umbrella to this woman?

2

Does this garden belong to the king? (belongs this garden etc.) **No,**
it belongs to the sister of the king. We have sold our horse to **the**
friend of our uncle. Does this knife belong to this or to that servant?

35.

Nom. ein Buch, a book;   eine Feder, a pen;
Dat. einem (i'-nem) Buche, to a book; einer (i'-ner) Feder, to a pen.

Der Vetter, fet'-ter, the cousin; die Base, bå'-zai, the female cousin; Amalie,
å-må'-lee-ai, Amelia; der Gärtner, gherrt'-ner, the gardener; die Gärtnerin, gherrt'-
ner-in, the gardener's wife.

Dieser Garten gehört einem Schuhmacher. Dieses Messer gehört
einer Magd. Luise hat meinem Vater einen Brief geschrieben. Hein=
rich hat meiner Mutter eine Blume gegeben. Ich habe Ihrem Onkel
mein Pferd geliehen. Sie haben unserer Tante ihr Haus verkauft.
Karl hat seinem Freunde ein Buch geschickt. Amalie hat ihrer Freundin
einen Fingerhut geliehen. Dieser Mann hat eurer Nachbarin einen
Vogel geschickt. Hast du meinem Vater diese Uhr gegeben? Habt ihr
unserer Base einen Bleistift geliehen?

36.

I have lent my pen to a friend of my brother. Hast thou given
thy cat to a friend (fem.) of my sister? We have given the letter
to a servant of the physician. Have you sent this flower to our
gardener? This garden belongs to my cousin (masc. and fem.). This
umbrella does not belong (belongs not) to your brother. Does this
pen belong (belongs this pen) to thy brother or to thy sister? Has
Henry written to his father or to his mother? Has Louisa written
to her uncle or aunt?

37.

Von, fon, of, from, by.

Of the mother, der Mutter, or von der Mutter;
of the child, des Kindes, or von dem Kinde;
of the father, des Vaters, or von dem Vater;
of this garden, dieses Gartens, or von diesem Garten;
of my sister, meiner Schwester, or von meiner Schwester.

Ich spreche, sprech'-chai, I speak, or I am speaking; wir sprechen, veer sprech'-chen,
we speak, we are speaking; wird geliebt, virrt gai-leept', is loved.

Obs. Of is expressed by the Genitive, when *of* relates to a substantive, and by von followed by the
Dative, when *of* relates to a verb.

Ich habe das Buch des Arztes gesehen. Haben Sie dieses Buch von
dem Arzte erhalten? Wir haben den Garten unsers Nachbars gekauft.
Haben Sie diesen Garten von Ihrem Nachbar gekauft? Ich habe diese
Uhr von meinem Onkel erhalten. Heinrich hat einen Brief von seinem
Vater und (von) seiner Mutter erhalten. Ich spreche von dem Könige
und der Königin. Wir sprechen von Ihrem Bruder und Ihrer Schwester,

von diesem Manne und dieser Frau. Sprechen Sie von meinem Vetter oder meiner Base? Heinrich wird von seinem Vater und seiner Mutter geliebt.

38.

I have received this horse from my friend. I have bought this cat of thy sister. Louisa has got an umbrella from her uncle and a watch from her aunt. I speak of this dog and of this cat, of this bird and of this flower. We are speaking of your cousin (masc. and fem.). Amelia is loved by her uncle and aunt. Our gardener's wife has received a letter from her son and daughter. Henry is the son of this shoemaker, and Louisa is the daughter of this tailor.

39.

Schön, beautiful; schöner, shö'-ner, more beautiful; der schönste, shö'n'-stai, the most beautiful;

gut, good; besser, better; der beste, bess'-tai, the best;

hoch, ho'ch, high; höher, hö'-her, higher; der höchste, hö'ch'-stai, the highest.

Das Thier, teer, the animal; der Löwe, lö'-vai, the lion; der Tiger, tee'-gher, the tiger; das Metall, mai-tâl', the metal; das Silber, sil'-ber, the silver; das Gold, gölt, the gold.

Obs. The Superlative is formed by adding ste or este to the Positive, and softening the radical vowel, i. e. changing a into ä, o into ö, and u into ü.

Die Katze ist nicht so stark, wie der Hund. Der Löwe ist stärker, als der Tiger. Der Löwe ist das stärkste Thier. Mein Nachbar ist reicher, als Sie; er ist der reichste Mann der Stadt. Das Gold ist schwerer, als das Silber. Das Eisen ist nützlicher, als das Silber. Das Eisen ist das nützlichste Metall. Luise ist schöner, als Amalie; aber Heinrich ist das schönste Kind. Ludwig ist jünger, als du; er ist der jüngste Sohn unsers Nachbars. Karl ist älter, als ich; er ist der älteste Sohn meines Onkels. Der Hund ist sehr treu. Der Hund ist das treueste Thier. Dieses Buch ist besser, als jenes. Du bist der beste Freund meines Bruders. Das Haus dieses Kaufmannes ist das höchste der Stadt.

40.

It is, es ist; that is, das ist.

This bird is very little; it is the smallest bird. Louisa is very beautiful; she is more beautiful than her sister. (The) silver is not as useful as (the) iron. The tiger is not as strong as the lion. The tailor is the happiest man in the town. Henry is more diligent than Lewis, but Charles is the most diligent. Thy umbrella is very beautiful; the umbrella of my cousin is the most beautiful. You are not as poor as my cousin; he is the poorest man in the town. My chair is too high; this one is higher; but the chair of my mother is the highest. I have given my brother the best pencil and the best pen.

41.

Nom. wer, vair, who?
Dat. wem, vaim, to whom?
Acc. wen, vain, whom?

Was, vâss, what; etwas, et'-vâss, something; nichts, nichts, nothing; Jemand, yey'-mânt, anybody, somebody; Niemand, nee'-mânt, nobody; hier, here, here; da, dâ, there.

Wer ift da? Es ift der Schneider; es ift Heinrich; ich bin es. Wer ift jener Mann? Es ift der Schufter; es ift der Sohn des Arztes. Wer hat diefen Brief gefchrieben? Wem gehört diefer Hund? Er gehört unferem Nachbar. Wem gehört diefe Uhr? Sie gehört meiner Schwefter. Wem haben Sie den Hut gegeben? Von wem haben Sie diefe Blume erhalten? Wen haben Sie gefehen? Was haben Sie verloren? Ich habe nichts verloren. Haben Sie etwas gefunden? Wo ift Ihr Bruder? Er ift nicht hier. Ift Jemand da? Es ift Niemand da. Hat Jemand meine Feder genommen? Niemand hat Ihre Feder genommen.

42.

Who is there? It is my tailor; it is Charles. Who is that woman? It is the wife of the shoemaker; it is the servant of the neighbor To whom have you lent your knife? To the son of the gardener. To whom has your brother sold his dog? To the sister of my friend. From whom hast thou received this bird? From the father of this girl. What have you bought? I have bought an umbrella for my cousin (fem.). What have you taken? I have taken nothing. Of whom do you speak? (fprechen Sie). I am speaking of nobody. Has anybody read my letter? Nobody has read your letter.

43.

Nom. welcher, welche, welches, vel'-cher, –ai, –ess,   who or which;
Dat. welchem, welcher, welchem, vel'-chem, –er, –em,   to whom or to which;
Acc. welchen, welche, welches, vel'-chen, –ai, –ess,   whom or which.

Der Schreiner, shrî'-ner, the joiner; gemacht, gai-mâcht, made; ausgegangen, ouss''-gai-gâng'-en, gone out; geweint, gai-vî'nt', cried, wept; in, in; mit, mit, with; bei, bi, with (at the house of).

Obs. The prepositions in, mit, bei govern the Dative. But in governs the Accusative, when the verb of the sentence denotes either motion or direction towards an object.

Welcher Schreiner hat diefen Tifch gemacht? Welche Magd hat diefen Brief gefchrieben? Welches Kind hat geweint? Welchen Hund haben Sie gekauft? Welche Uhr haft du verloren? Welches Haus hat Ihr Vater verkauft? Von welchem Volke fprechen Sie? Mit welchem Freunde bift du ausgegangen? In welchem Garten hat er den Vogel gefunden? Welche Feder haft du da? Welcher Frau haft du dein Meffer gegeben? Welchem Mädchen haft du deinen Fingerhut geliehen? Bei welchem Kaufmann haben Sie diefen Bleiftift gekauft? Mit welcher Feder haben Sie diesen Brief geschrieben? Mit wem sind Sie angekommen?

44.

Where is your sister? She is in her garden. Where is your brother? He is with (at the house of) his friend. Is your father gone out? He is gone out with the physician. Which hat have you bought? Which book have you read? Which pen have you taken? Which boy is the most diligent? Which watch is the best? From which gardener hast thou received this flower. At the house of (bei) which woman hast thou bought this bird? In which house have you lost your thimble? With whom is your brother departed? To which man have you lent your umbrella? Which stick have you lost? Which joiner has made this table?

45.

Der Apfel, åp'-fel, the apple; die Birne, birr'-nai, the pear; gegessen, gai-gess'-sen, eaten.

Obs. In those sentences, which begin with a relative pronoun, the verb is placed at the end.

Wir haben einen Bruder, welcher sehr groß ist. Ihr habt eine Schwester, welche sehr klein ist. Mein Sohn hat ein Buch, welches sehr nützlich ist. Der Garten, welchen dein Onkel gekauft hat, ist sehr schön. Die Feder, welche mein Vetter gefunden hat, ist sehr gut. Ich habe das Haus gesehen, welches Ihr Vater gekauft hat. Haben Sie den Fingerhut gefunden, welchen meine Schwester verloren hat? Hast du den Apfel gegessen, welchen du gefunden hast? Ich habe die Birne gegessen, welche ich gekauft habe. Hier ist der Mann, welchem Sie Ihren Brief gegeben haben. Hier ist die Frau, welcher wir unsern Hund verkauft haben. Hier ist der Arzt, von welchem wir so oft sprechen.

46.

Obs. Instead of welcher, etc., may be used der, die, das; for instance: der Apfel, den or welchen er gegessen hat.

I have a dog which is very little. We have a cat which is very fine. My father has bought a house which is very beautiful. Have you seen the umbrella which my mother has bought? Hast thou found the pear which thy brother has lost? We have seen the horse which your uncle has sold. Where is the thimble which you have found? I have taken the pencil which my cousin has bought. Henry has eaten the apple which his brother has received. Have you seen the woman of whom we speak? Have you read the letter which I have written? Have you found the boy to whom this penknife belongs?

47.

Derjenige, welcher, dair''-yai'-nig-ai vel'-cher,	he who;
diejenige, welche, dee''-yai'-nig-ai vel'-che,	she who;
dasjenige, welches, dâss''-yai'-nig-ai vel'-chess,	that which.

Obs. Instead of derjenige, etc., may also be used der, die, das ; for instance : der, welcher.

Derjenige, welcher zufrieden ift, ift reich. Diefer Fingerhut ift beffer, als derjenige meiner Schwefter. Diefe Uhr ift kleiner, als diejenige deines Bruders. Diefes Haus ift schöner, als dasjenige unfers Nach=bars. Ich habe meinen Hut verloren und den meines Vetters. Wir haben deine Feder gefunden und die deines Freundes. Heinrich hat mein Zimmer gefehen und das meines Onkels. Haft du meinen Stock genommen oder den meines Bruders? Das ift nicht deine Blume, das ift die meiner Mutter. Haben Sie mein Meffer oder das des Gärt=ners? Sprechen Sie von meinem Sohne oder von dem des Arztes? Das Pferd, welches wir gekauft haben, ift jünger, als dasjenige Ihres Vaters.

48.

He who is rich, is not always contented. My dog is more faithful than that of my uncle. Our servant is stronger than that of our neighbor. My room is larger than that of my friend. This um-brella is finer than that which we have bought. Have you taken my pen or that of my sister? This is not your pencil; it is that of my brother. I speak of my book and of that of your friend. Louisa has lost her thimble and that of her mother. Thou hast eaten my apple and that of my cousin. My watch is better than that of my cousin (fem.). I have received your letter and that of your brother.

49.

Heinrich, Henry;	Luife, Louisa;
Heinrichs, Henry's;	Luifens, Louisa's;
dem Heinrich, to Henry;	der Luife, to Louisa;
von Heinrich, of or from Henry;	von Luifen, of or from Louisa.
Wilhelm, vil'-helm, William;	Aachen, â'-chen, Aix-la-Chapelle;
Johann, yo-hân', John;	Brüffel, brüss'-sel, Brussels;
Emilie, ai-mee'-lee-ai, Emily;	heißt, hi'sst, is called;
Wien, veen, Vienna;	geht, gheyt, goes;
Köln, köln, Cologne;	wohnt, vo'nt, lives.

Er heißt Karl, his name is Charles.

The hat of Henry, der Hut Heinrich's; to Brussels, nach Brüffel; at Brussels, zu or in Brüffel.

Mein Bruder heißt Heinrich und meine Schwefter heißt Luife. Der Vater Wilhelms ift angekommen. Die Mutter Luifens ift abgereift. Ludwigs Onkel ift fehr reich. Emiliens Hut ift fehr schön. Haben Sie diefen Hund von Heinrich oder von Ferdinand erhalten? Amalie hat dem Johann ihre Feder geliehen. Karl hat der Emilie eine Blume gegeben. Gehört dieser Garten dem Ludwig oder der Karoline? Wo ist Wilhelm? Er ist mit Karl und Joseph ausgegangen. Wohnt Ihr Onkel in Brüssel oder in Paris? Geht Ihr Vetter nach Wien oder nach Berlin? Ist Paris größer, als Lyon? Ist Ihr Freund von Köln oder von Aachen?

Obs. The proper names of persons are declined with or without an article. If declined with the article, they remain unchanged. Without the article the feminine names ending in e add n# in the Genitive and n in the Dative.

50.

My cousin's name is John. The daughter of our gardener's wife is called Jane (Johanna). Art thou Charles' or Ferdinand's brother? Where are Henry and Lewis? They are in my father's room; they are gone out with William. Have you lent your pen to Henry? Who has given this flower to Louisa? We have received a letter from Lewis; he is at Dusseldorf. The sister of Charles is very short. The bonnet of Josephine is too large. My uncle lives in Vienna and my cousin in Paris. My friend goes to Cologne. William is arrived from Amsterdam. Have you seen John and Lewis? My garden is larger than that of Emily. Louisa is gone out with her mother. Henry is departed with his friend Ferdinand.

PART II.

51.

Nom. die Tische, the tables;
Gen. der Tische, of the tables
Dat. den Tischen, to the tables;
Acc. die Tische, the tables.

Obs. 1. Nouns of one syllable take e in the plural. Those nouns whose radical vowel is a, o, u, au, generally change them into ä, ö, ü, äu. As: die Magd, mähdt, the female servant — die Mägde, maid'-tai, the female servants; der Sohn, zone, the son — die Söhne, zö'-nai, the sons; der Hut, hoot, the hat — die Hüte, hü'-tai, the hats; der Traum, troum, the dream — die Träume, troi'-mai, the dreams.
Obs. 2. The Dative plural of all nouns terminates in n.

Die Freunde meines Vaters sind angekommen. Die Söhne unsers Nachbars sind sehr fleißig. Die Stühle, welche wir gekauft haben, sind sehr schön. Haben Sie die Städte Wien und Berlin gesehen? Karl hat die Hüte Wilhelms und Ferdinands gefunden. Mein Vater hat die Briefe Ihres Onkels nicht erhalten. Das Eisen und das Silber sind Metalle. Die Pferde sind nützlicher, als die Hunde. Die Mägde eures Nachbars sind sehr fleißig. Die Aerzte in dieser Stadt sind sehr reich. Wem haben Sie die Stöcke meines Bruders gegeben? Die Thiere, welche wir in Ihrem Garten gesehen haben, sind sehr stark.

Haben Sie den Freunden Heinrichs geschrieben? Gebet diesen Hund
den Söhnen meines Bruders. Wir sprechen von den Briefen des Arztes.

52.

Thy brother has bought the dogs of my neighbor. The friends of
Charles are ill. Have you seen the horses of our uncle? Who has
written the letters of my brother? Where are the hats that you
have bought? I have received this bird from the sons of the physician. I have given your umbrella to the maid-servants. (The)
metals are very useful. (The) dogs are very faithful. Your brother
is gone out with the sons of our neighbor (fem.). Cologne and Aix-
la-Chapelle are towns. I speak of Henry's and William's friends.

53.

Der Zahn, tsåhn, the tooth;　　　der Ring, ring, the ring;
der Fuß, fooss, the foot;　　　die Nuß, nööss, the nut;
die Hand, hånt, the hand;　　　der Baum, boum, the tree;
der Schuh, shoo, the shoe;　　　warm, wårrm, warm;
der Strumpf, ströömpf, the stocking;　　rein, rine, clean; weiß, vice, white.

Obs. The pronouns: dieser, jener, welcher, mein, dein, sein, unser, euer, ihr take in the plural the same terminations as the articles der, die, das.

Meine Zähne sind sehr weiß. Ich habe die Füße sehr warm. Ihre
Hände sind nicht rein. Hat der Schuster meine Schuhe gebracht? Wer
hat meine Strümpfe genommen? Sind das Ihre Strümpfe? Das
sind nicht die meiner Schwester. Wo haben Sie diese Nüsse gekauft?
Haben Sie meine Bäume schon gesehen? Von welchen Bäumen sprechen Sie? Von denjenigen, welche ich von dem Gärtner der Königin
gekauft habe. Unsere Freunde sind schon abgereist. Wer hat diese Briefe
geschrieben? Mein Vater hat seine Pferde und Hunde verkauft. Mein
Nachbar hat einen Brief von seinen Söhnen erhalten, welche in Berlin
sind. Hat Jemand meine Ringe gefunden? Niemand hat deine Ringe
gesehen. Karl wird von seinen Freunden geliebt.

54.

Their, ihr; those, diejenigen or die.

*Charles and Henry have lost their sticks. The shoemaker has
not made your shoes. Where have you bought these tables and
chairs? From whom have you received these pencils? My feet are
very small. My sister has lost her thimbles. I have received these
letters from my friends. These trees are higher than those. These
animals are very fine. These servants are very lazy. Have you
already seen our hats and our rings? Emily's stockings are whiter
than those of Louisa. Your teeth are not clean. My hands are
very warm. I have found these nuts in my uncle's garden.

55.

Alle, al'-lai, all.

Das Kind, the child;		das Dorf, dorrf, the village;
das Buch, the book;		das Blatt, blât, the leaf;
das Haus, the house;		das Loch, loch, the hole;
das Volk, the people;		das Huhn, hoon, the chicken;
das Glas, glâhss, the glass;		das Kalb, kâlp, the calf;
das Band, bânt, the ribbon;		der Wurm, vöörm, the worm;
das Kleid, klite, the dress;		der Wald, vâlt, the forest;
das Schloß, shloss, the castle;		der Mann, mân, the husband.

Obs. All these monosyllabical nouns are exceptions from the general rule, and form their plural by adding **er**, and softening the radical vowel. Nouns ending in **thum** follow the same rule, as: Irrthum, irr'-toom — Irrthümer, irr'-tü-mer (mistake).

Diese Häuser sind höher, als jene. Jene Bänder sind schöner, als diese. Deine Bücher sind nützlicher, als die Luisens. Diese Mutter hat ihre Kinder verloren. Der König hat seine Schlösser verkauft. Von wem haben Sie diese Gläser erhalten? Wer hat diese Kleider gemacht? Dieser Mann ist schon sehr alt; er hat alle seine Zähne verloren. Wo sind Ihre Freunde? Alle meine Freunde sind ausgegangen. Diese Völker sind sehr glücklich; sie haben einen König, welcher sehr gut ist. Die Könige sind nicht immer glücklich. Heinrich und Wilhelm haben alle ihre Bücher verloren. Alle eure Briefe sind angekommen. Wir haben alle diese Nüsse in dem Walde unsers Onkels gefunden. Der Vater ist mit allen seinen Kindern abgereist. Diese Dörfer sind sehr schön. Von welchen Dörfern sprechen Sie? Welche Städte haben Sie gesehen? Sind alle diese Strümpfe für Luisen oder für Emilien? Haben Sie den Kindern des Nachbars einen Vogel gegeben? Wer hat alle diese Löcher in meinen Tisch gemacht?

56.

● Not yet, noch nicht.

Where are your children? My children are gone out. Their friends are arrived. Have you not yet written your letters? Who has bought all these ribbons? Henrietta has lost all these books. We have seen all these houses. Have you also seen the castles of the king? Who has taken all my nuts? These children have lost their hats. Give these glasses to Henry and these rings to Louisa. This tree has lost all its leaves. My neighbor has sold all his chickens.

57.

Der Stiefel, stee'-fel, the boot;		der Kutscher, kööt'-sher, the coachman;
der Spiegel, spee'-ghel, the mirror;		der Schuster, shoo'-ster, the shoemaker;
der Löffel, löf'-fel, the spoon;		das Mädchen, mait'-chen, the girl;
die Nadel, nâ'-del, the needle;		der Engländer, eng'-len-der, the Englishman,
die Gabel, gâ'-bel, the fork;		der Italiener, ee-tâ-lee-ai'-ner, the Italian.

Obs. Masc. and neuter substantives ending in **er, el, en**, do not change in the plural; the feminine nouns ending in **er**, and **el** take **n**, except: die Mütter, the mothers; die Töchter, the daughters; der Vetter the cousin, die Vettern.

2*

Die Schneider und Schuster in dieser Stadt sind alle reich. Die Eng=
länder sind sehr fleißig. Meine Brüder sind alle krank. Haben Sie
meine Schwestern gesehen? Wo haben Sie diese Messer, Löffel und
Gabeln gekauft? Die Fenster Ihres Zimmers sind offen. Karl und
Heinrich sind meine Vettern. Wir haben diese Vögel in dem Walde
gefunden. Die Tiger sind sehr stark. Diese Mädchen sind sehr glücklich.
Sind meine Töchter ausgegangen? Sind meine Zimmer nicht sehr
schön? Hat Ihre Tante alle diese Spiegel gekauft? Wer hat die
Bücher und Federn dieses Mädchens genommen? Wem gehören diese
Gärten und Häuser? Luise und Henriette haben ihre Nadeln verloren.
Der Schuster hat Ihre Schuhe und Stiefel noch nicht gebracht. Wer
sind jene Männer? Es sind Italiener; es sind die Onkel meines Freun=
des. Diese Mütter sind sehr traurig; sie haben alle ihre Kinder verloren.

58.

The shoemaker has brought your shoes and boots. The houses of
this village are all very fine. Bring us (bringen Sie uns) the spoons,
forks and knives. Where have you bought these needles? Your
brothers and sisters are not come. Lewis and Ferdinand are cousins.
Our mothers have seen the gardens of the king. My sons have
bought the mirrors of my neighbor. (The) horses are bigger than
(the) tigers. Are my stockings clean? Are your shoes new?

59.

Eins (ein), i'nss, ine, one;	sechzehn, zech'-tsain, sixteen;
zwei, tsvi, two;	siebenzehn, zee'-ben-tsain, seventeen;
drei, dri, three;	achtzehn, ächt'-tsain, eighteen;
vier, feer, four;	neunzehn, noin'-tsain, nineteen;
fünf, fünf, five;	zwanzig, tsvân'-tsich, twenty;
sechs, zecks, six.	die Aufgabe, Auf''-gâ'-bai, the task, exercise;
sieben, zee'-ben, seven;	das Jahr, yâhr, the year;
acht, ächt, eight;	die Woche, voch'-chai, the week;
neun, noin, nine;	der Monat, mo'-nâht, the month (pl. -e);
zehn, tsain, ten;	der Tag, tâhch, the day;
eilf, i'lf (elf), eleven;	die Stunde, stôôn'-dai, the hour;
zwölf, tsvölf, twelve;	der Knabe, k'nâ'-bai, the boy;
dreizehn, dri'-tsain, thirteen;	seit, zite, since (Dat.);
vierzehn, feer'-tsain, fourteen;	es gibt, gheept, es ist, there is;
fünfzehn, fünf'-tsain, fifteen;	es gibt, es sind, there are;

gemacht, gai-mâcht', made, done.

Obs. Nouns ending in e take n in all the cases of the plural.

In unserm Hause sind vierzehn Zimmer. In diesem Zimmer sind
zwei Tische und zwölf Stühle. Unser Nachbar hat fünf Kinder: drei
Söhne und zwei Töchter. Wir haben vier Katzen und drei Hunde. In
eurem Garten sind fünfzehn Bäume. Das Jahr hat zwölf Monate;
der Monat hat vier Wochen; die Woche hat sieben Tage. Ich habe von
meinem Vater sechs Aepfel und acht Birnen erhalten. Mein Onkel hat

meiner Schwester ein Federmesser und zwanzig Federn gegeben. Haft
du schon alle deine Aufgaben gemacht? Johann hat noch nicht seine
Aufgabe gemacht. Mein Bruder ist schon drei Jahre in Berlin. Haben
Sie noch nicht gegessen? Ich habe schon seit drei Stunden gegessen.
Ist Ihr Vater noch nicht angekommen? Er ist schon seit zwei Tagen
angekommen. Mein Onkel ist seit vier Wochen krank; er hat seit acht
Tagen nichts gegessen. Mein Bruder ist neun Jahre alt, aber meine
Schwester ist noch nicht sieben Jahre alt.

60.

My father has three houses and two gardens. This man has five
boys and four girls. My friend has seven sisters. We have received
six letters. In this town there are twenty physicians. My cousins
(fem.) have bought two cats. My cousin is seventeen years and two
months old. My mother has bought six knives, twelve forks and
eighteen spoons. Our joiner has made three tables and ten chairs.
We have received this week fifteen chickens and three calves. William has eaten five apples, four pears and eleven nuts. Henry is
arrived three days ago (since three days). My uncle is departed a
twelvemonth ago (since a year). Charles and Ferdinand have made
exercises. There are two holes in this door. The gardener has given
three flowers to my children.

61.

Das Brot, brote, the bread;   Brot, some or any bread;
das Fleisch, fli'sh, the meat;   Fleisch, some meat;
die Aepfel, ep'-fel, the apples;   Aepfel, some apples;

Der Wein, vine, the wine;   die Pflaume, pflou'-mai, the plum,
das Bier, beer, the beer;   die Dinte, din'-tai, the ink;
das Wasser, vàss'-ser, the water;   die Suppe, sööp'-pai, the soup;
das Gemüse, gai-mü'-zai, the vegetables;   man findet, mån fin'-det, one finds, they
der Zucker, tsöök'-ker, the sugar;   find;
der Kaffee, kàf'-fai, the coffee;   getrunken, gai-tröönk'-en, drunk;
geben Sie mir, gai'-ben zee meer, give me;   bringen Sie uns, bring'-en zee ööns,
die Kirsche, kirr'-shai, the cherry;   bring us.

Ich habe Brot und Fleisch gegessen. Wir haben Kirschen und Pflaumen gekauft. Mein Bruder hat Wein getrunken und ihr habt Bier und
Wasser getrunken. Der Schuster macht Schuhe und Stiefel. Der
Schreiner macht Tische und Stühle. Bei diesem Kaufmann findet man
Bücher, Federn, Dinte und Bleistifte. Geben Sie mir Suppe und Gemüse. Hier ist Wein und Wasser, und da ist Kaffee und Milch. Haben Sie auch Zucker? Wir haben Messer und Gabeln, Tassen und Gläser gekauft. Der Gärtner hat der Luise Kirschen und Blumen gegeben.
Haben Sie schon Kaffee getrunken? In jenem Hause findet man Spiegel, Regenschirme, Bänder, Fingerhüte und Nadeln. Meine Freundin

hat von ihrem Onkel Birnen und Nüffe erhalten. Wir haben Löwen, Tiger, Katzen und Hunde gesehen. In diefer Stadt gibt es Schneider und Schufter, welche fehr reich find.

62.

Wollen Sie? vol'-len see, will you (have)? gefälligft, gai-fel'-lichst, if you please.

Will you have some wine or some beer, some milk or some water? Give me, if you please, some soup, vegetables, meat and bread. Where does one find (finds one) ink and pens? Are you a father? Have you children? Has your father bought any trees or flowers? My brother has books and friends. Here is coffee and sugar. My neighbor has birds, dogs and horses. We are speaking of towns and villages, of houses and gardens. Iron and silver are metals. Vienna and Berlin are towns. What have you made? We have done exercises (Aufgaben gemacht), we have written letters. We have eaten apples and plums, and we have drunk some wine and beer.

63.

Wenig, vai'-nich, little, few; | zu, tsoo, to, too; wie? vee, how?
viel, feel, much; | das Obft, o'pst, die Frucht, frööcht, the fruit;
viele, fee'-lai, many; | das Geld, ghelt, the money;
genug, gai-nooch', enough; | der Pfeffer, pfef'-fer, the pepper;
mehr, mair, more; | das Salz, zälts, the salt;
weniger, vai'-nig-er, less, fewer; | der Senf, zenf, the mustard.

Heinrich hat viel Geld; er hat mehr Geld, als ich. Geben Sie mir ein wenig Fleifch. Ich habe genug Brod. Du haft zu viel Salz und Pfeffer. Wir haben weniger Obft, als ihr. Luife hat weniger Federn, als Henriette. Karl hat mehr Aufgaben gemacht, als Ludwig. Haft du fo viel Geld, wie mein Bruder? Der Arme hat wenig Freunde. Es gibt wenig Menfchen, welche zufrieden find. Geben Sie der Henriette nicht zu viel Senf. Mein Bruder hat zu viel Wein getrunken. Diefe Mutter hat viele Kinder. Diefer Mann hat viele Blumen. Wie viele Hunde hat Ihr Vater? Es gibt diefes Jahr wenig Kirfchen, aber viele Pflaumen. Mein Freund hat diefe Woche mehr Briefe erhalten, als ich. Hat dein Vater fo viele Bücher, wie mein Onkel? Geben Sie mir gefälligft ein wenig Dinte. Wollen Sie noch mehr? Ich habe genug.

64.

There is much fruit this year. Our gardener has many trees and flowers. Will you have a little meat or some vegetables? Have you mustard enough? I have salt and pepper enough. Our neighbor has much money; he is very rich. Give a little wine to this woman. This man has few friends, but he has many dogs and cats. There are many birds in this forest. How many physicians are there in your town? Have you as many apples and pears as we? We have

not so many as you, but we have more plums and nuts than you.
Charles has fewer friends than Henry. This tree has fewer leaves
than that one. There are too many chairs in this room.

65.

Das Stück, stück, the piece;
die Flasche, flâsh'-shai, the bottle;
die Tasse, tâss'-sai, the cup;
das Pfund, pföönd, the pound;
die Elle, el'-lai, the yard, ell;
das Paar, pâhr, the pair;
das Dutzend, dööt'-sent, the dozen;
der Korb, korrp, the basket;

die Leinwand, line'-vânt, the linen;
das Taschentuch, tâsh''-shen-tooch', the
  pocket-handkerchief;
der Handschuh, hânt'-shoo, the glove;
das Hemd, hemt, the shirt;
die Halsbinde, hâlss'-bin-dai, the cravat;
der Käse, kai'-zai, the cheese;
der Schinken, shink'-en, the ham.

Obs. The words Pfund, Paar and Dutzend are invariable when they are preceded by a number. — The
English word *of* which follows the names of weights and measures is not expressed in German.

Meine Mutter hat der Henriette drei Paar Handschuhe, sechs Paar
Strümpfe, zwei Dutzend Hemden und einen Korb Kirschen geschickt.
In diesem Koffer sind zehn Ellen Leinwand, vier Taschentücher und sechs
Halsbinden. Mein Bruder hat zwei Paar Schuhe und ein Paar Stie=
fel gekauft. Wir haben dem Freunde unseres Onkels zwanzig Pfund
Zucker und zehn Flaschen Wein geschickt. Geben Sie mir ein Stück Käse,
eine Flasche Bier und ein wenig Senf. Ich habe ein Glas Wein ge=
trunken und ein Stück Schinken gegessen. Wir haben bei unserer Freun=
din eine Tasse Kaffee getrunken. Geben Sie mir ein Glas Wasser und
ein Stück Zucker. Meine Schwester hat zwei Pfund Kirschen und ein
Pfund Pflaumen gekauft. Wir haben ein Dutzend Stühle bei dem
Schreiner unseres Onkels gekauft. Ich habe von dem Gärtner einen
Korb Blumen erhalten.

66.

The shoemaker has made a pair of shoes for Louisa and two pair
of boots for William. We have 'drunk two glasses of wine and three
glasses of beer. Give me a bottle of water and a little meat and
bread. Will you have a piece of ham or cheese? My aunt has
bought a dozen'of cravats, two dozen of shirts and ten pair of gloves
and stockings. How many shirts have you? I have three dozen.
This linen is very fine; how many yards have you bought? I have
bought twenty yards. That is not enough for ten shirts. My uncle
has given to Henry a penknife, twenty pens, two cravats and a pair
of gloves. Ferdinand has bought a pound of plums, six pounds of coffee and two yards of ribbon. Give me, if you please, a glass of water.

67.

Sing. guter, gute, gutes, goo'-ter, –tai, –tess; *Plur.* gute, goo'-tai.

Schlecht, shlecht, bad;
kalt, kâlt, cold;
hübsch, hüpsh, pretty ·
todt, tote, dead;

vortrefflich, fore-treff'-lich, excellent;
liebenswürdig, lee''-bens-vürr'-dich, amiable;
das Papier, pâp-peer', the paper;
das Geschäft, gai-sheft', the affairs, business.

Obs. If the adjective is not preceded by an article or such words, as: biefer, jener, welcher, derfelbe, derjenige, it takes the termination of biefer, e, es.

Hier ist guter Schinken, gute Suppe und gutes Brot. Haben Sie gutes Papier und gute Dinte? Wir haben schlechten Wein und gutes Bier getrunken. Unser Gärtner hat vortreffliches Obst. Unsere Magd hat guten Senf, aber schlechten Pfeffer gekauft. Eduard hat gute Freunde und nützliche Bücher. Mein Onkel hat schöne Gärten und große Häuser. Euer Nachbar hat treue Hunde. Johann, geben Sie mir ein Glas Wasser! Wollen Sie kaltes oder warmes Wasser? Meine Schwester hat ein Paar hübsche Handschuhe gekauft. Euer Bruder spricht immer von gutem Wein und guter Suppe, aber nicht von nützlichen Büchern, von Aufgaben und Geschäften. Paris und London sind schöne Städte. Heinrich hat ein Paar neue Schuhe erhalten.

68.

Have you any good mustard? We have good bread and good meat. Your gardener has very fine flowers. These children have fine dresses. We have faithful friends, amiable brothers and useful Books. Give me some better cheese and better beer. At (bei) this merchant's one finds pretty gloves, fine penknives, and good pens. Iron and silver are very useful metals. You have always excellent wine. My brother is not gone out, he has too many affairs. Henry has bought good paper and good ink. We speak of good coffee, of excellent fruit and new dresses.

69.

Ein guter, eine gute, ein gutes.

Golden, gol'-den, golden; gesund, gai-zoont', healthy, wholesome;
silbern, zil'-bern, of silver; kein, kine, no, none.

Obs. If the adjective is preceded by the indefinite article, by kein or by a possessive pronoun, as: mein, dein, unfer, etc., it takes in the Nominative Sing. the terminations er, e, es, and in all other cases en, except the Accusative fem. and neuter, which is the same as the Nominative.

Unser Gärtner ist ein guter Mann. Eure Gärtnerin ist eine gute Frau. Emilie ist ein gutes Kind. Wir haben einen guten Vater und eine gute Mutter. Heinrich hat ein schönes Pferd und einen schönen Hund. Luise hat große Zähne, aber eine kleine Hand und einen kleinen Fuß. Ferdinand ist mit meinem jüngern Bruder ausgegangen. Henriette ist mit meiner ältern Schwester abgereist. Geben Sie dieses Brot einem armen Kinde. Dieses Federmesser gehört einem jungen Manne, der bei unserm Nachbar wohnt. Ludwig ist der Sohn eines reichen Kaufmanns. Haben Sie guten Wein oder gutes Bier? Wir haben keinen guten Wein und kein gutes Bier. Wer hat meine silberne Uhr und meinen goldenen Ring genommen? Wir haben unsern besten Freund verloren. Eure kleinen Kinder sind sehr gesund. Es gibt keine guten Kirschen dieses Jahr. Mein Onkel hat seine schönsten Pferde verkauft.

Biſt bu mit denen neuen Stiefeln zufrieden? Haſt bu ſchon von unſern guten Pflaumen gegeſſen?

70.

Charles is a good boy. Henrietta is a pretty girl. That is a happy mother. That is an excellent wine. Where is my little Henry, my good Louisa? We have a very rich uncle. William has an old father. Iron is a useful metal. The dog is a faithful animal. I have received a new umbrella and a golden watch. My neighbor has done much business this year. Give this bottle of wine to a poor man or to a poor woman. I have no friend in this town. Have you no good pens for this child? Our best friends are dead. This joiner makes no good chairs.

71.

Der gute, bie gute, bas gute.

Heute, hoi'-tai, to-day;   ber Schüler, shü'-ler, the pupil, school-boy;
bie Schule, shoo'-lai, the school;   bas Leben, lai'-ben, the life;
                          ich liebe, lee'-bai, I love, I like.

Obs. When the adjective is preceded by the definitive article or words like bieſer, jener, etc., it takes in the Nominative Sing. the final e, and in all other cases en, except the Accusative Sing. fem. and neuter.

Der gute Heinrich iſt krank. Die kleine Sophie iſt ſehr liebenswür= big. Das arme Kind hat ſeine Mutter verloren. Das iſt der höchſte Baum in unſerm Garten. Liſette iſt die fleißigſte von unſern Mägden. Dieſer reiche Engländer wohnt bei meinem Onkel. Wo haben Sie dieſe goldene Nadel gefunden? Wem gehört dieſes große Haus und jener ſchöne Garten? Franz iſt mit dem kleinen Karl ausgegangen. Wir haben geſtern bei der guten Emilie Kirſchen gegeſſen. Wer wohnt in dieſem ſchönen Schloſſe? Wie heißt dieſe hübſche Blume? Wo haben Sie dieſen ſchlechten Wein und dieſes ſchlechte Bier gekauft? Ich liebe die fleißigen Schüler und die treuen Freunde. Der Löwe und der Tiger ſind die ſtärkſten Thiere. Das ſind die glücklichſten Tage meines Lebens. Geben Sie dieſem armen Manne ein wenig Wein. Leihen Sie dieſem kleinen Mädchen Ihren Regenſchirm.

72.

Every one, Jebermann, yey''-der-mân'.

The diligent pupil is loved by every one. The idle child is loved by nobody. The good king is loved by his people. This poor woman has no bread for her children. This rich merchant has given much money to the poor. I like the pretty flowers and the pretty children. I do not like the fine dresses. This fruit is not wholesome. My brother has found this gold ring to-day. Lewis is gone out with his little brother. The father of this young man is a shoemaker. The daughter of this old woman is ill. Have you drunk of this excellent wine? Will you (have) some of these fino plums? Which hat have you taken? I have taken the white hat. Which watch have you sold? I have sold the silver watch.

73.

Der erſte, eyr'-stai, the first;
ber zweite, tsvi'-tai, the second;
ber britte, drit'-tai, the third;
ber vierte, feer'-tai, the fourth;
ber leßte, lets'-tai, the last;
    ber wievielſte, vee-feel'-stai, what day of the month?

unartig, ŏŏn''-âhr'-tiĉ, naughty;
beſcheiben, bai-shi'-den, modest;
ber Theil, tile, the part;
ber Banb, bânt, the volume;
bie Klaſſe, klâss'-sai, the class;
nur, noor, only.

Obs. *Of* before the name of a month is not expressed in German.

Dieſer junge Mann iſt ſehr fleißig; er iſt ber erſte in ber Klaſſe. Karl iſt ber zweite; ber beſcheibene Heinrich ber britte; Johann iſt ber vierte; ber kleine Wilhelm iſt ber fünfte; Paul iſt ber ſechſte; Franz iſt ber achte; Guſtav iſt ber neunte; ber unartige Eduarb iſt ber elfte unb ber faule Lubwig iſt ber leßte. Zwei iſt ber fünfte Theil von zehn. Fünf iſt ber vierte Theil von zwanzig. Ein Tag iſt ber ſiebente Theil einer Woche. Den wievielſten beś Monatś haben wir heute? Wir haben heute den breizehnten ober ben vierzehnten. Iſt eś nicht ber zwanzigſte? Mein Vater iſt ben britten Mai abgereiſt. Mein Onkel iſt ben zehnten December angekommen. Haben Sie ben erſten unb zweiten Banb? Ich habe nur ben erſten.

74.

Louisa is the first in the class; Maria is the second; the good Josephina is the third, Henrietta is the fifth; the modest Sophia is the ninth; Matilde (Mathilbe) is the fifteenth; the naughty Caroline is the last. Three is the sixth part of eighteen. A week is the fourth part of a month; and a month is the twelfth part of a year. What day of the month is it (have we)? It is to-day the eleventh or the twelfth. We departed on the second of May and arrived on the sixteenth. Which volume have you taken? Have you taken the third and the fourth? I have only taken the third.

75.

Singular.   *Plural.*

Der meinige, mi'-nig-ai, bie meinige, baś meinige, mine;   bie meinigen;
ber beinige, di'-nig-ai, thine;   ber unſrige, ŏŏn'-zrig-ai, ours;
ber ſeinige, zi'-nig-ai, his;   ber eurige, oi'-rig-ai, Ihrige, ee'-rig-ai, ours;
ber ihrige, ee'-rig-ai, hers: ber ihrige, theirs;
                              leicht, li'ĉt, easy, light.

Obs. Instead of: ber meinige, etc., may be said: meiner, meine, meineś or meinś, with the terminations of bieſer, bieſe, bieſeś. — The declension of ber meinige, berjenige, etc., is the same as that of the adjective, preceded by the definite article.

Dein Vater iſt größer, alś der meinige. Meine Mutter iſt kleiner, alś bie beinige. Unſer Buch iſt nüßlicher, alś baś Ihrige. Mein Sohn ist nicht so alt, als der deinige. Euer Pferd ist jünger, als das unsrige. Unsere Bücher sind nützlicher, als die eurigen. Mein Vater hat seine Uhr verloren; Heinrich hat auch die seinige verloren. Meine Schwester hat die ihrige verkauft. Mein Vater hat deinen Brief und den meinigen gelesen. Meine Tante hat ihren Garten und den unsrigen verkauft. Hat dein Bruder meinen Stock oder den seinigen genommen? Hat Luise meinen Fingerhut oder den ihrigen gefunden? Deine Aufgaben sind leichter, als die meinigen. Diese Bäume sind höher, als die unsrigen. In unsrer Stadt sind mehr Aerzte, als in der eurigen.

76.

My thimble is as fine as yours. Your umbrella is not so large as mine. My son is more diligent than thine. My friend has sold his house and mine. My sister has eaten her apple and thine. Has Louisa taken my pen or hers; my pencil or hers? Henry has read my books and yours. Your sisters are younger than ours. We speak of our friend and of yours. Is my room smaller than thine? I have promised a book to your son and to mine, to your daughter and to mine. I speak of my tasks and of thine. This castle belongs to my uncle and to yours.

77.

Singular.	Plural.
Nom. er, air, he; sie, zee, she; es, ess, it;	sie, they;
Accus. ihn, een, him; sie, her; es, it;	sie, them.

Gehabt, gai-hápt', had;   gebracht, gai-bráct', brought;
ja, yáh, yes;   nein, nine, no.

Haben Sie meinen Stock? Ja, ich habe ihn. Haben Sie meine Uhr? Nein, ich habe sie nicht. Haben Sie mein Messer? Ich habe es nicht. Haben Sie meine Schuhe? Ja, ich habe sie. Wo ist mein Hund? Ich habe ihn nicht gesehen. Wer hat meine Feder genommen? Dein Bruder hat sie genommen. Wo hast du dieses Taschentuch gefunden? Ich habe es in Ihrem Zimmer gefunden. Diese Vögel sind sehr schön. Von wem hast du sie erhalten? Deine Schwester ist sehr fleißig; meine Mutter liebt sie sehr. Haben Sie meinen Oheim gekannt? Ich habe ihn nicht gekannt. Dies ist ein nützliches Buch; haben Sie es schon gelesen? Wo ist mein Fingerhut? Ich habe ihn Ihrer Schwester gegeben; sie hat ihn verloren. Hat Jemand meine Gabel genommen? Karl hat sie genommen. Wem hat der Gärtner alle diese Blumen geschickt? Er hat sie Ihrer Mutter geschickt. Hat Heinrich deinen Bleistift gehabt? Nein, er hat ihn heute nicht gehabt.

78.

Has the shoemaker brought my boot? Yes, he has brought it. Hast thou already done thy task? I have not yet done it.

you seen my new room? No I have not yet seen it. Where hast thou bought these pretty rings? I have bought them in Paris. Who has had my penknife? I have not had it, your brother has had it. I have received a letter of my aunt, have you read it? Have you already seen the king? I have not yet seen him. You have a good pen; lend it to my sister. There is your brother; do you not see him? Where are your gloves? Lend them to your aunt. Where is your umbrella? Give it to this child. My aunt is dead; did you know her? Which books have you there? Have you read them? Where is thy dog? My father has sold it.

79.

Ich bin gewesen, gai-vai'-zen, I have been;
du bist gewesen, thou hast been;
er ist gewesen, he has been;
wir sind gewesen, we have been;
ihr seid gewesen, you have been;
sie sind gewesen, they have been.

Herr, herr, Mr.;
der Herr, the gentleman;
die Frau, frou, woman, wife, lady;
Madame, mâ-dâm', Madam, Mrs;
Fräulein, froi'-line, Miss;
das Fräulein, the young lady;

die Dame, dâ'-mai, the lady;
der Morgen, morr'-ghen, the morning;
das Viertel, feer'-tel, the quarter;
lange, lang'-ai, long, a long time;
zusammen, tsöö-zäm'-men, together;
ein halber, e, es, hâl'-ber, –bai, –bess, half a.

Das erste Mal, mâhl, the first time; das letzte Mal, the last time; ein Mal, once; zwei Mal, twice.

Obs. The word Herr takes in all cases of the Singular n, and in all cases of the Plural en. It is also used with the article in the sense of Mr. — In speaking politely, the words Herr, Frau and Fräulein are used as a title, as in French, for instance: Ihr Herr Vater, your father; Ihre Frau Mutter, your mother; Ihre Fräulein Schwestern, your sisters.

Wer ist hier gewesen? Herr Moll ist hier gewesen; er hat dieses Buch gebracht. Bist du bei dem Schuster gewesen? Ich bin heute bei deinem Schuster gewesen; er hat Ihre Stiefel schon gemacht. Wo seid ihr diesen Morgen gewesen? Wir sind bei unserm Freunde Karl gewesen, welcher sehr krank ist. Dieser Herr ist drei Jahre in Wien gewesen, und seine Brüder sind sehr lange in Konstantinopel gewesen. Du bist nicht fleißig gewesen, du hast deine Aufgabe noch nicht gemacht. Ich bin gestern bei Madame Röder gewesen; sie ist eine sehr liebenswürdige Frau. Ist Fräulein N. oft in dieser Stadt gewesen? Sie ist schon drei Mal hier gewesen. Haben Sie den Herrn Scholl gekannt? Ich habe ihn in Berlin gekannt; wir sind oft zusammen ausgegangen. Wie lange sind Sie in Madrid gewesen? Ich bin nur ein halbes Jahr da gewesen, aber ich bin drei Viertel Jahr in Lissabon gewesen. Haben Sie die Herren Nollet schon gesehen? Ich habe sie gestern bei einem meiner Freunde gesehen.

80.

Have they (has one) brought my shoes? Yes, they have brought them. Has the tailor been here? No, he has not yet been here. Hast thou been at the joiner's? No, I have not been there. We have many flowers; we have been in the garden of (the) Mr. Nollet. Have you also been at Mr. Moll's? My brother has never been more contented than to-day; he has received from his uncle a beautiful gold watch, and half a dozen pocket-handkerchiefs. How long have you been in Paris? We have been there six months. These Gentlemen have done much business; they have been very lucky. Have Messrs. N. already departed for Cologne? They departed this morning with their uncle; I saw them at Mrs. Sicard's.

81.

Jd) war, vâhr, I was;   wir waren, vâ'-ren, we were;
bu warft, vâhrst, thou wast;   ihr waret, vâ'-ret, you were;
er war, vâhr, he was;   fie waren, vâ'-ren, they were.

Ehemals, ey''-hai-mâhlss', formerly; warum, why; als, âlss, when.

Obs. When a sentence begins with als, when, the verb is placed at the end of the phrase.

Wo warft bu biefen Morgen? Jd) war bei meinem Better, weldher von Frankfurt angekommen ift. Mein Bruder unb id), wir waren bei beinem Bater. Jhre Tante war fdhon abgereift. Herr Moll war ehemals fehr reidh; er hat feit zehn Jahren viel verloren. Waren Sie nodh nidht bei Herrn Mably? Jd) bin geftern ba gewefen, aber er war ausgegangen. Wie alt war ihr Bruder, als er in Köln war? Er war zehn ober elf Jahre alt. Wir waren nidht zufammen; er war in Köln unb id) war in Düffelborf. Meine Sdhweftern waren lange in Brüffel bei Herrn Nollet. Warum finb Sie geftern nidht gekommen? Jd) war geftern krank. Waren biefe Herren immer fo reidh? Haben Sie immer fo viele Freunbe gehabt? Warft bu biefen Morgen in ber Sdhule? Jd) bin heute nidht in ber Sdhule gewefen.

82.

I was formerly much happier; I was young and strong. Wast thou always as contented as to-day? My father was formerly very rich. You were gone out, when I came (I am come). Where were you, when we (are) arrived? My sisters were very ill yesterday, How old were you, when you were at N.? I was fifteen years and six months old. Was my room open, when you came (you are come)? No, but the windows were open. This girl was much prettier, when she was young. John and William were always my brother's friends. Were you not with my brother, when he (has) lost his handker

83.

Ich hatte, hât'-tai, I had;   wir hatten, hât'-ten, we had;
du hattest, hât'-test, thou hadst;   ihr hattet, hât'-tet, you had;
er hatte, hât'-tai, he had;   sie hatten, hât'-ten, they had.

Die Eltern, el'-tern, the parents; der Besuch, bai-zooch', the visit; der Handel, hân'-del, the commerce, trade; der andere, ân'-dai-rai, the other; die Kaufleute, kouf''-loi'-tai, merchants, purchasers.

Obs. Nouns compound with Mann usually take Leute, instead of Männer, in the plural.

Wir hatten diese Woche den Besuch der Herren Moll, welche mit ihrer Schwester angekommen sind. Ihr hattet viele Freunde, als ihr noch jung waret. Wir hatten mehr Bücher, als ihr. Unser Onkel hatte ehemals viele Pferde und Hunde. Du warst sehr fleißig, als du noch deine Eltern hattest. Diese zwei Kaufleute waren ehemals sehr reich; sie hatten einen großen Handel. Ich hatte zwei Brüder; der eine war in Wien, der andere in Berlin. Hast du meine zwei Brüder gekannt? Ich habe denjenigen gekannt, welcher in Berlin war; der andere war jünger, als ich. Wo ist euer Vetter, der so viele Vögel hatte? Er ist seit einem Jahre in Brüssel. Mein Federmesser war verloren; Ihr Bruder hat es gefunden. Hattet ihr eure Briefe schon geschrieben, als wir ausgegangen sind? Wir hatten sie noch nicht geschrieben; wir hatten keine guten Federn und kein gutes Papier.

84.

Der Verstand, fer-stânt', the intellect; die Güte, gü'-tai, the kindness.

Mr. Maury was formerly much happier, he had many friends, much money, many horses and dogs. Henry is dead; he was a good boy, he had so much intellect and kindness, he was loved by every body. We were often in his garden; his sisters were very amiable, and they had many flowers and books. His parents were not rich, but they had a great trade. I was ill yesterday; I had eaten too much fruit. Hadst thou not yet done thy exercises when I came (I am come)? No, I had not yet done them. My brother had already done his, when thou camest (art come).

85.

Mir, meer, to me, me;   ihm, eem, to him, him;
dir, deer, to thee, the;   ihr, eer, to her, her.

Kaufen, kou'-fen, to buy;   schreiben, shri'-ben, to write;
verkaufen, ferr-kou'-fen, to sell;   lesen, lai'-zen, to read;
geben, gai'-ben, to give;   sehen, zey'-hen, to see;
leihen, li'-hen, to lend;   (die) Lust, lôôst, a mind;
thun, toon, to do;   die Zeit, tsite, the time;
machen, mâch'-chen, to make, to do;   das Vergnügen, fer-g'nü'-ghen, the pleasure.

Ich kann, kân, I can;   wir können, kön'-nen, we can;
du kannst, kânst, thou canst;   ihr könnet, kön'-net, you can;
er kann, kân, he can;   sie können, kön'-nen, they can.

Obs. The Infinitive is placed at the end of the sentence.

Kannst du mir dieses Buch leihen? Ich kann dir dieses Buch nicht leihen; es gehört meinem Vetter Heinrich. Wer kann diesen Brief lesen? Ich kann ihn lesen; er ist sehr gut geschrieben. Wir können diesen Morgen nicht schreiben. Warum können ihr nicht schreiben? Wir haben keine Tinte. Können Sie meinem Bruder Ihre Uhr leihen? Ich kann ihm meine Uhr nicht leihen, ich habe sie dem Herrn S. verkauft. Haben Sie meiner Schwester eine Feder gegeben? Ich habe ihr keine Feder gegeben. Haben Sie Lust, diesen Hund zu kaufen? Ich habe keine Lust, ihn zu kaufen; er ist nicht treu. Hat Ihr Bruder heute nichts zu thun? Er hat drei Briefe zu schreiben. Wir haben noch zwei Aufgaben zu machen. Ich habe gestern das Vergnügen gehabt, Ihre Fräulein Schwester zu sehen. Haben Sie Zeit, diesen Brief zu lesen? Ich habe jetzt nicht Zeit, ihn zu lesen. Können Sie mir einen Regenschirm geben? Ich kann Ihnen keinen geben, ich habe nur einen. Ihr Herr Bruder hat die Güte, mir den seinigen zu leihen. Sind Sie gestern bei meiner Tante gewesen? Nein, ich war gestern nicht bei ihr; ich hatte zu viele Geschäfte.

86.

Can you do that? Yes, I can (it); but my brother cannot. Will you lend me your penknife? I cannot lend thee my penknife; my sister has taken it. Have you given a pen to my cousin? Yes, I have given him one. Hast thou sold thy dog to my sister? I have not sold her my dog. Canst thou not do thy exercise? I cannot do it to-day. We can read this book. These gentlemen cannot write their letters; they have no paper. Hast thou a mind to buy a pair of boots? Has your brother a mind to sell his ring? Have you had the kindness to give a glass of water to this poor man? My friend has had the pleasure to see his parents. I have not had time to read all these letters. My father has had the kindness to buy me a golden watch. Hast thou seen it? I have not yet seen it. Have you been with Ferdinand to-day? I have been with him this morning.

87.

Uns, to us, us; euch, Ihnen, to you, you; ihnen, to them, them.

Gehen, ghey'-hen, to go;
kommen, kom'-men, to come;
trinken, trink'-en, to drink;
essen, ess'-sen, to eat;

haben, hâ'-ben, to have;
sein, zine, to be; wenn, ven, if;
unwohl, ŏŏn'-vo'l, indisposed;
jetzt, yetst, now, at present.

Ich will, vill, I will;
du willst, villst, thou wilt;
er will, he will;

wir wollen, vol'-len, we will,
ihr wollet, vol'-let, you will;
sie wollen, they will.

Willst du mit mir gehen? Ich kann nicht mit dir gehen, ich habe keine Zeit. Ich will dir ein schönes Buch leihen, wenn du fleißig

bift. Kann dein Bruder heute nicht kommen? Er hat keine Luſt zu
kommen; er iſt unwohl. Wir wollen jetzt unſere Aufgabe machen.
Wollen Sie ein Glas Wein trinken? Ich habe ſchon ein Glas Bier
getrunken. Ich will ein Stück Fleiſch oder Käſe eſſen. Wollen Sie
ein wenig Senf und Salz? Können Sie uns dieſen Stock leihen?
Ich kann Ihnen dieſen Stock nicht leihen, mein Bruder will ihn
haben. Man kann nicht unglücklicher ſein, als dieſer junge Mann;
er hat ſeine Eltern und ſeine Brüder und Schweſtern verloren. Wer
will dieſen Apfel haben? Ich will ihn haben. Was willſt du jetzt
thun? Ich will ein paar Briefe ſchreiben. Ich will euch einen Korb
Kirſchen geben, wenn ihr fleißig ſein wollet. Wollen Sie die Güte
haben, mir eine Nadel zu geben? Ich habe jetzt keine, ich kann Ihnen
keine geben. Haben Sie Zeit, mit uns zu gehen? Ich habe keine
Zeit, mit Ihnen zu gehen. Haben Sie den Herren N. ſchon einen
Beſuch gemacht? Ich habe ihnen dieſen Morgen einen Beſuch gemacht.

88.

What hast thou to do? I have nothing to do. Wilt thou read
this book? Yes, I will read it. How is thy brother? He is indisposed, he cannot come. Where can one buy these fine penknives?
One can buy them at the merchant's who lives at our neighbor's.
Will you give me a little ink? Can your sister lend me her penknife? What do these gentlemen want (what will etc.)? These ladies
will buy an umbrella. One cannot be more unhappy than I (am);
one cannot have more misfortune than I. Give us something to
drink. What will you (have)? Will you have wine or beer? I have
lent you my stick. Where are your brothers? I have sold them my
dog. This man is very rich; all these houses belong to him.

89.

Mich, mich, me, myself;   dich, dich, thee, thyself;
uns, öönss, us, ourselves;   euch, oich, you, yourselves;
    ſich, zich, one's self, him-, her-, itself, themselves.

Loben, lo'-ben, to praise;   gelobt, gai-lo'pt', praised;
lieben, lee'-ben, to love, like;   geliebt, loved;
beſuchen, bai-zoo'-chen, to visit;   beſucht, bai-zoocht, visited;
ſchlagen, ſhlä'-ghen, to beat;   geſchlagen, gai-ſhlä'-ghen, beaten;
ſich ſchlagen, to fight;   der Lehrer, ley'-rer, the master;
waſchen, väſh'-shen, to wash;   gewaſchen, gai-väſh'-shen, washed.

Der Lehrer hat dich gelobt, weil du fleißig geweſen biſt. Dein
Bruder iſt ein böſer Knabe; er hat mich geſtern geſchlagen. Haſt du
dich ſchon gewaſchen? Ich habe mich noch nicht gewaſchen; aber
Heinrich hat ſich ſchon ſeit einer Stunde gewaſchen. Warum willſt
du meinen Hund ſchlagen? Er hat mein Brot genommen. Unſere
Eltern ſind unſere beſten Freunde; wir wollen ſie immer lieben. Karl

du bist sehr unartig; man kann dich nicht lieben. Wie viele Gläser Wein hast du getrunken? Ich habe nur eine halbe Flasche getrunken. Wo bist du diesen Morgen gewesen? Ich bin mit meinem Vater bei Herrn N. gewesen. Ist Herr N. noch immer unwohl? Er ist seit gestern ein wenig besser; aber er kann noch nicht essen noch trinken. Der Arzt war heute zweimal bei ihm. Ich will ihn morgen auch besuchen, oder ihm einen kleinen Brief schreiben. Aber warum haben Sie uns noch nicht besucht? Ich habe noch keine Zeit gehabt, Sie zu besuchen.

90.

Who has beaten thee? Your cousin has beaten me. With whom wilt thou fight? I will not fight. I have no mind to fight. Lewis will fight with Henry. The servant has not yet washed my shirts. She will wash them now. I have sold you my penknife, but you have not yet given me the money. Your children have been very good (artig) to-day; the master has praised them very (much); he has given them a beautiful book, and a basket of cherries. Why has the master not yet visited us? He has no time; he is always in his school. He is an amiable man; he is loved by all his pupils. There is Ferdinand; hast thou washed thyself, my child? Yes, mamma (Mama), I have already washed myself.

91.

Sagen, zå'-ghen, to say, to tell;	glauben, glou'-ben, to believe;
schicken, shick'-ken, to send;	wissen, vis'-sen, to know.

Müssen, müss'-sen, must.

Ich muß, mõõss, I must;	wir müssen, we must;
du mußt, mõõst, thou must;	ihr müsset, müss'-set, you must;
er muß, he must;	sie müssen, they must.

Obs. The Accusative of the personal pronoun is placed before the Dative.

Können Sie mir sagen, wo Herr Moll wohnt? Ich kann es Ihnen nicht sagen. Wollen Sie mir diese Feder leihen? Ich kann sie Ihnen nicht leihen, sie gehört mir nicht. Ich muß heute dem Fräulein S. einen Besuch machen, sie ist gestern mit ihrer Mutter angekommen. Mußt du jetzt schon gehen? Wo sind meine Schuhe? Hat der Schuster sie noch nicht gebracht? Nein, er will sie dir in einer Stunde schicken. Wie kannst du das wissen? Er hat es mir gesagt. Ich kann es nicht glauben. Dein Bruder muß noch seine Aufgaben machen. Wir müssen Alles thun, was unsere Eltern und Lehrer wollen. Ihr müsset meinen Vetter einmal besuchen; er ist seit drei Wochen krank. Heinrich und Wilhelm müssen viele Bücher haben. Wer hat dir diesen Ring gegeben? Meine Tante hat ihn mir gegeben. Luise, ich will dir etwas sagen; du hast ein Loch in deinem Strumpf. Ich habe es schon gesehen, Mutter. Wollen Sie meiner Schwester biesen Fingerhut geben? Ich will ihn ihr jetzt geben. Wer hat Ihnen biesen Brief geschrieben? Meine Base hat ihn mir geschrieben.

92.

My friend has had the kindness to send me a basket of cherries. You have not yet sent me my book. I have not yet had time to send it you. Who has taken my pen? I cannot tell (it) thee. Wilt thou not believe me? This penknife belongs to my brother; thou must give it him. Charles will not lend me his umbrella. Why will he not lend it thee? My uncle is arrived. Your brother has told (it) us. Who must do that? Your sisters must do it. You must tell it to Mr. Moll. This letter is not well written; I cannot read it. Hast thou my stick? No, I have it not. I have lent it to you. You have not lent it to me.

PART III.

93.

Ich lobe, lo'-bai, I praise, I am praising, I do praise;
bu lobest, lobst, lo'-best, lo'pst, thou praisest, etc.;
er lobet, lobt, lo'-bet, lo'pt, he praises;
wir loben, lo'-ben, we praise;
ihr lobet, lobt, lo'-bet, lo'pt, you praise;
sie loben, lo'-ben, they praise.

Wohnen, vo'-nen, to live, to dwell;   bas Tuch, tooch, the cloth;
bringen, hring'-en, to bring;   bie Straße, strä'-sai, the street;
ber Buchhändler, booch''-hend'-ler, the bookseller;   ber Thaler, tä'-ler, dollar.

Was suchen Sie? Ich suche meine Feder. Mein Bruder sucht seinen Bleistift. Wir suchen unsern Hund. Diese Kinder suchen ihre Bücher. Wo kaufen Sie Ihr Papier? Wir kaufen unser Papier bei dem Buchhändler. Ich finde meinen Stock nicht. Wer hat meinen Stock genommen? Ich glaube, daß Ihr Bruder ihn genommen hat. Ich liebe biesen Knaben nicht, er ist immer unartig. Du liebst beinen Lehrer. Gott liebt bie guten Menschen. Gute Kinder lieben ihre Eltern. Ist es wahr, daß Ihr Onkel sein Haus verkauft? Wie theuer ver= kaufen Sie die Elle von biesem Tuche? Ich verkaufe die Elle bieses Tuches zu vier Thaler. Das ist sehr theuer. Findest du nicht, Hein= rich, baß das sehr theuer ist? Ja, ich finde es sehr theuer. Wir ver= kaufen aber viel von biesem Tuche. Jedermann findet es schön. Schicken

Sie mir drei und eine halbe Elle. Wissen Sie, wo ich wohne? Ja,
Sie wohnen in der Petersstraße. Meine Magd kann es Ihnen heute
noch bringen.

94.

Tabeln, tá'-deln, to blame;
arbeiten, árr'-bi-ten, to work;

Alles, ál'-less, all, every thing,
Alles was, all that.

What are you doing? I am reading the book, which your brother
has lent me. You read too much. Why do you not write? I have
already written three letters. My cousins never write. You always
blame your cousins; one must blame nobody. What art thou doing?
I am doing my exercise. What is thy sister doing? She is working.
What do you drink? I drink wine and my brother drinks beer.
We drink no wine. I eat cherries. My brothers eat plums. You
are always eating, but you do not work. Can you tell me, where
Mr. N. lives? He lives in (the) William's street. Livest thou with
thy uncle? No, I do not live with him. Dost thou go to Paris?
No, I do not go to Paris. I do not like this young man; he always
blames his friends. He will never lend me his penknife. I lend him
all that I have. We lend every thing to our friends. You always
beat my brother; you are very naughty. These boys beat every
body. Do you sell paper? I sell paper, pens and ink. What do
you say? I say, that you have taken my knife.

95.

Ich lobte, lo'p'-tai, I praised, I did praise, I was praising;
du lobtest, lo'p'-test, thou praisedst, etc.;
er lobte, lo'p'-tai, he praised;
wir lobten, lo'p'-ten, we praised;
ihr lobtet, lo'p'-tet, you praised;
sie lobten, lo'p'-ten, they praised.

Spielen, spee'-len, to play;
lachen, lâch'-chen, to laugh;
tanzen, tân'-tsen, to dance,
erzählen, er-tsai'-len, to tell, relate;
theilen, ti'-len, to share, divide;
erlauben, er-lou'-ben, to allow, permit;
suchen, zoo'-chen, to seek, look for.

die Geschichte, gai-shich'-tai, the story;
der Abend, â'-bent, the evening;
so sehr, zo zeyr, so much;
ganz, gânts, quite, whole;
bis, biss, til, until;
daß, dâss, that;

Obs. The adverb **so**, which connects two sentences, is not translated in English.

Dein Bruder und ich, wir wohnten zu N. in dem nämlichen Hause.
Wir waren den ganzen Tag zusammen. Wir machten unsere Aufgaben zusammen, wir spielten zusammen und hatten kein größeres Vergnügen, als wenn wir zusammen waren. Er liebte mich und ich liebte
ihn so sehr, daß wir wie Brüder waren. Wenn dein Vater ihm etwas
schickte, so theilten wir es. Ich arbeitete oft für ihn und er arbeitete
für mich. Der Lehrer lobte und liebte uns. Alle gute Schüler waren

3*

unsere Freunde; sie besuchten uns jeden Tag; wir erzählten uns schöne Geschichten und lachten und tanzten, bis es Abend war. Du schicktest uns oft hübsche Bücher, welche uns viel Vergnügen machten. Wir hatten sehr oft Zeit zu lesen. Wenn wir unsere Aufgaben gemacht hatten, erlaubte der Lehrer uns immer zu spielen oder ein nützliches Buch zu lesen.

96.

Wählen, vai'-len, to choose;	das Spiel, speel, the play, game;
weinen, vi'-nen, to cry, to weep;	während, vai'-rent, while, during.

Obs. The Nominative is always placed after its verb, in a sentence, which serves to complete the preceding one: wenn er kommt, gehe ich mit ihm.

When we were young, we lived in this house. Your sister bought some ribbons and chose the finest for you. Formerly I loved play, but at present I love books. This people always loved their king. Thy cousin was still looking for his hat, when we (are) departed. The merchant, whom thou soughtest yesterday, has been here. Thy brother has sold his penknife this morning. While we were crying, you were laughing and dancing. My father allowed me always to read good books and to play with my friends. We often worked together, when you were living with your uncle. I danced better than you, but you did your exercises better than I. Thou wast often idle, and thou hadst not always a mind to read and to write. I told thee pretty stories, but thou lovedst play too much, thou didst play the whole day. The master blamed thee often, and the good scholars did not love thee.

97.

Ich werbe, verr'-dai, loben, I shall or will praise;
du wirst, virrst, loben, thou wilt praise;
er wird, virrt, loben, he will praise;
wir werden, verr'-den, loben, we shall praise;
ihr werbet, verr'-det, loben, you will praise;
sie werden, verr'-den, loben, they will praise.

Obs. Werben, taken in an absolute sense, signifies *to become;* but when constructed with another verb, it answers to the English auxiliary verb *shall* or *will.*

Ich werde diesen Abend das Vergnügen haben, meinen Onkel zu sehen. Ich werde dir diesen hübschen Ring geben, wenn du fleißig sein wirst. Heinrich wird mir heute ein Paar schöne Handschuhe kaufen. Deine Schwester wird zufrieden sein, wenn sie ihre Aufgabe gemacht hat. Wenn wir in N. sein werden, werden wir viel Vergnügen haben. Wann werden Sie mich besuchen? Ich glaube, wir werden Sie morgen besuchen. Meine Brüder werden auch heute oder morgen kommen. Es wird meinem Vater sehr viel Vergnügen machen, sie noch einmal zu sehen. Wann werden Sie Ihrem Freunde Karl schreiben? Ich schreibe ihm in acht bis vierzehn Tagen. Wollen Sie die Güte haben, mir das

Buch zu schicken, welches Sie mir versprochen haben? Ich werde es Ihnen heute schicken, Fräulein. Mein Bedienter wird es Ihnen bringen. Ich hatte es einem Freunde geliehen, der es bis jetzt gehabt hat.

98.

Das Wetter, vet'-ter, the weather; hierher, here'-hair, hither; der Bediente (–ter), bai-deen'-tai (–ter), the man servant, valet.

Shall you go with us? I do not believe, that my father will allow me (allows it to me). Has the shoemaker brought my boots? No, he will bring them to you this evening. What shall we do now? We will drink a glass of wine. Will you have the kindness to lend me your horse? I shall lend it you with much pleasure. We shall play to-day in the garden of our uncle; he will allow (it) us. I shall tell you a beautiful story, if you are good and diligent. Wilt thou work to-day? I believe that I shall not work to-day. Come hither, my children; you will be very tired. If your cousins are departed, they will have fine weather. Thy exercise is badly done; the master will blame thee. All (the) scholars will go to N. to-day. Charles, thou must wash thyself, if thou wilt go with Henry. Yes Mamma, I shall wash myself at present.

99.

Ich würde, vürr'-dai, loben, I should or would praise;
du würdest, vürr'-dest, loben, thou wouldst praise;
er würde, vürr'-dai, loben, he would praise;
wir würden, vürr'-den, loben, we should praise;
ihr würdet, vürr'-det, loben, you should praise;
sie würden, vürr'-den, loben, they would praise.

Wenn ich hätte, het'-tai, if I had; wenn ich wäre, vai'-rai, if I were; gern, gherrn, willingly; ob, op, if.

Obs. After the conjunctions wenn and ob, if, the Subjunctive Mood is used in German, when the verb is in the Imperfect or in the Pluperfect tense.

Ich würde glücklicher sein, wenn ich Bücher und Freunde hätte. Ich würde mehr Vergnügen haben, wenn meine Vettern hier wären. Du würdest nicht so reich sein, wenn du nicht so viele Geschäfte gemacht hättest. Wenn Heinrich Geld hätte, würde er diese Messer kaufen. Ich würde deinen Bruder besuchen, wenn ich Zeit hätte. Du würdest diesen Hund nicht so sehr lieben, wenn er nicht so treu wäre. Wir würden dich nicht tadeln, wenn du fleißiger gewesen wärest. Dein Onkel sagte mir, du würdest morgen nicht kommen. Welchen von diesen Stöcken würdest du wählen? Wem würdet ihr eure Blumen geben? Was würdest du sagen, wenn ich meinen Hund verkaufte? Ich würde dir erlauben zu spielen, wenn du deine Aufgaben gemacht hättest. Diese Kinder würden sehr weinen, wenn ihre Mutter abgereist wäre. Dein

Vater würde uns eine schöne Geschichte erzählen, wenn wir artiger ge=
wesen wären. Wenn du Zeit zu lesen hättest, würde ich dir ein nützli=
ches Buch leihen. Ich würde gern mit dir gehen, aber mein Lehrer
will es nicht erlauben; ich muß heute noch drei Briefe schreiben.

100.

Louisa would be very (much) pleased, if she had all these flowers.
Henry would not have so many friends, if he were not so kind (gut)
and good (artig). We should not yet have (be) come, if we·had not
received a letter from our father. We should not have sold our
house, if my father had done more business (pl). The master would
blame thee, if thou hadst not done thy exercise. I should not believe
it, if thou hadst not seen it. If we had an apple, we should share
it. We should go with you, if we were not so tired. If I had some
money, I should buy a pound of cherries. If you loved me, I should
love you also. If you told me, where Mr. N. lives, I would give you
a glass of wine. Would you believe that I have done this? Would
you do me this pleasure, if I allowed you to play this evening? I
would do it willingly, if I had time.

101.

Ausgehen, ouss'-ghey-hen, to go out.

Ich gehe aus, ghey'-hai ouss, I go out;
du gehst, gheyst, aus, thou goest out;
er geht, gheyt, aus, he goes out;
wir gehen, ghey'-hen, aus, we go out;
ihr gehet, ghey'-het, aus, you go out;
sie gehen, ghey'-hen, aus, they go out.

Aufmachen, ouf-''mäch'-chen, to open;
zumachen, tsoo''-mäch-chen, to shut;
zurückschicken, tsoo-rück''-shik'-ken, to
   send back;
angenehm, än''-gai-naim', agreable,
   pleasant;

die Nachricht, näch'-richt, the news;
abschreiben, äp''-shri'-ben, to copy;
mittheilen, mit''-ti'-len, to communicate;
anziehen, än''-tsee'-hen, to put on;
schwarz, shwärrts, black;
früher, frü'-her, earlier, sooner.

Obs. The compound verbs are formed by the addition of a particle which modifies the sense of the
simple verb, and which is detached from it in the Present and Imperfect tenses of the Indicative Mood,
unless the sentence begins with a conjunction or a relative pronoun.

Ich gehe heute nicht aus; das Wetter ist zu schlecht. Mein Bruder
will auch nicht ausgehen. Wenn das Wetter schöner wäre, würden wir
gern ausgehen. Heinrich, du machst nie die Thüre zu. Kannst du
diese Kommode aufmachen? Ich mache mein Zimmer zu, wenn ich aus=
gehe. Ich schicke Ihnen diesen Abend das Buch zurück, welches Sie
mir geliehen haben. Mein Vetter schickte mir gestern den Stock zurück,
den ich ihm geliehen hatte. Schreibst du alle diese Briefe ab? Mußt
du alles das abschreiben? Ich schreibe nur so viel ab, als ich will. Ich
würde diese Aufgabe noch abschreiben, wenn mein Lehrer es mir erlaubte.

Ich muß Ihnen etwas mittheilen. Was wollen Sie mir mittheilen? Ich theile Ihnen eine angenehme Nachricht mit. Warum theilten Sie mir das nicht früher mit? Welches Kleid ziehst du heute an? Ich ziehe mein schwarzes Kleid an und meine Schwester wird ihr weißes Kleid anziehen. Wo ist das Kleid, welches Sie anziehen? Hier ist es.

102.

Die Gewohnheit, gai-vone'-hite, the habit; aufstehen, ouf"-stey'-hen, to get up; der Spaziergang, spât-seer'-gânk, the walk; weggehen, vech"-ghey'-hen, to go away; einen Spaziergang machen, to take a walk.

Do you not yet get up? No, I am indisposed; I shall not get up to-day. You always get up very late, that is a bad habit. I go away; I have much to do. I shall also go away. The weather is so fine, that I have a mind to take a walk. Shut the door, if you please. Open the window. Your brother always opens the door and the windows. Do you not go out to-day? I shall not go out to-day. My father wishes (will) it not. My brother goes out twice every day. I shall send you back your umbrella to-morrow. Send me also back the cane, which I have lent you. What is my son doing? He copies the letters which you have written this morning. My uncle is arrived; I shall communicate to him the good news. Put on your new dress; Mr. N. comes to see (visits) us to-day.

103.

Betrügen, bai-trü'-ghen, to deceive;
beleibigen, bai-li'-dig-en, to offend;
verlieren, fer-lee'-ren, to lose;
verbessern, fer-bess'-sern, to correct, improve;
verbieten, ferr-bee'-ten, to forbid;
erziehen, err-tsee'-hen, to bring up;
erhalten, err-hâl'-ten, to receive;

zerreißen, tser-ri'-sen, to tear;
warten, vârr'-ten, to wait;
anwenden, ân"-ven'-den, to employ;
zurückgeben, tsoo-rück"-gai'-ben, to give back;
die Gesellschaft, gai-zel'-shâft, the company;
die Sorgfalt, zorch'-fâlt, the care;
sogleich, zo-gli'ch, immediately, at once.

Obs. The syllables be, ge, ent, er, ver and zer serve to form the *derivative* verbs, and are not detached from the simple verb.

Dieser Kaufmann ist ein Betrüger, er betrügt Jedermann. Man muß Niemand betrügen. Wir betrügen Niemand. Du beleibigst mich immer. Dein Vetter beleibigte gestern die ganze Gesellschaft. Warum beleibigen Sie diesen Mann? Ich erhalte heute einen Brief von meinem Freunde in Köln. Wir erhalten alle Tage Nachricht von unserm Vater. Ich werde morgen Geld erhalten. Diese Mutter erzieht ihre Kinder mit vieler Sorgfalt. Wenn wir wollen, daß unsere Kinder gut werden, müssen wir sie mit Sorgfalt erziehen. Was suchst du, Karl? Ich habe meinen Ring verloren. Du verlierst immer etwas. Komm, wir müssen gehen, wir können nicht länger warten; du kannst den Ring später suchen. Gehen Sie nur, ich komme sogleich; ich werde den Ring finden. Warum zerreißest du dieses Papier? Das Papier ist mein, ich kann es zerreißen. Ich verbiete dir, es zu zerreißen. Willst du die Güte haben, mir meine Aufgaben zu verbessern? Dein Bruder verbesserte mir immer meine Aufgaben, als er noch hier war. Wann geben Sie mir meinen Bleistift zurück? Deine Brüder geben nie zurück, was man ihnen leiht. Wendet eure Zeit gut an. Man muß seine Zeit immer gut anwenden.

104.

I will not wait (any) longer. I lose my time. Shall you play today? No, we shall not play, we always lose. You would not lose, if you played better. We should play better, if we played oftener. If I receive my money, I shall play once more (noch einmal). Does your father not forbid you to play? Yes, he does forbid (it) us. This child is very naughty; he tears his dresses. My neighbor brings up his children very badly. I do not like this young man; he always offends me. Henry corrects his exercise; he employs his time well. He who employs well his money, is wise (weise). If you give me back my pencil, I shall give you back your pen. One must always give back, what is lent us (what one lends us).

105.

Wohnen, vo'-nen, to dwell;   gewohnt, gai-vo'nt, dwelt, been dwelling;
beleidigen, to offend;   beleidigt, bai-li'-digt, offended;
anwenden, ân''-ven'-den, to employ;   angewendet, ân''-gai-ven'-det, employed;
                der Augenblick, ou''-ghen-blick', moment.

Obs. The past Participle of simple verbs is formed by the addition of the initial syllable **ge**, and the final syllable **et** or **t**. In compound verbs **ge** is placed after the particle; the derivative verbs take only the final **et** or **t**.

' Haben Sie Ihre Aufgabe schon verbessert? Ich habe sie noch nicht verbessert; ich werde sie sogleich verbessern. Ihr Bruder hat mich gestern beleidigt; ich will nichts mehr mit ihm zu thun haben; von heute (an) ist er mein Freund nicht mehr. Wir wollen einen Spaziergang zusammen machen. Ich kann in diesem Augenblicke nicht ausgehen; ich habe diesen Morgen schon einen Spaziergang gemacht. Warum haben Sie mir mein Federmesser noch nicht zurückgegeben? Wer hat die Thüre aufgemacht? Wer hat Ihnen diese Nachricht mitgetheilt? Ihr Vater hat uns gestern eine artige Geschichte erzählt. Meine Mutter hat mir erlaubt, diesen Abend nach N. zu gehen. Sind Sie gestern bei meinem Vetter gewesen? Ja, wir haben den ganzen Tag bei ihm gespielt, gelacht und getanzt. Aber habt ihr auch gearbeitet? Ich glaube es nicht; der Lehrer hat dich schon mehrere Male getadelt, deine Schwester hat es mir oft gesagt. Wer hat euch diesen Korb Kirschen geschickt? Hast du deinen kranken Freund noch nicht besucht? Mein Onkel hat ein neues Pferd gekauft; er hat das alte dem Kutscher unseres Nachbars für zwanzig Thaler verkauft.

106.

Einzig, ine'-tsich, single, only; nicht mehr, no more; Sache, zäch'-chai, Ding, ling (dink), thing.

Thou hast employed thy time very badly, my dear Henry. I see that thou hast not done a single exercise. I have always praised thee, but I shall praise thee no more. Have you played together, my children? Yes, mamma, we have been playing and working. That is very well (gut); I shall give you some cherries and plums. I will divide them. We have divided them already. Why have you shut all (the) windows? The weather is so fine; I shall open them. Who has copied these letters? I believe that Henry has copied them. Have you been waiting long? We have waited (for) half an hour. Mr. N. has sent back the umbrella, which you had lent him. I have received a letter from my aunt which I have not yet opened. Your cousin is arrived; he has told us (a) hundred things. One must not believe all that he tells. I have not believed all.

107.

Um ... zu, ööm .... tsoo, in order to, to;
um zu loben, in order to praise, to praise;
um anzuwenden, in order to employ.

Wünschen, vün'-shen, to wish; abreisen, äp''-ri'-zen, to depart, set out; gefällig, gai-fel'-lich, obliging; sondern, zon'-dern, but (after a negative phrase).

Obs. The preposition zu, which generally precedes the Infinitive, is placed in the compound verbs between the particle and the verb.

Ich komme, um dir zu sagen, daß ich morgen abreise. Ich habe meinen Bedienten geschickt, um mir ein Pfund Tabak zu kaufen. Wir leben nicht, um zu essen, sondern wir essen, um zu leben. Um glücklich zu sein, muß man zufrieden sein. Um Freunde zu haben, muß man gefällig sein. Ich habe nicht Zeit, auszugehen. Haben Sie die Güte, diese zwei Briefe abzuschreiben. Wollen Sie so gut sein, die Thüre aufzumachen? Wir haben Lust, einen kleinen Spaziergang zu machen. Mein Nachbar hat zwei Pferde zu verkaufen. Wer hat dir erlaubt, so früh wegzugehen? Ist es noch nicht Zeit, aufzustehen? Ich habe das Vergnügen gehabt, den Herrn Moll zu sehen. Wünschen Sie mit meinem Vater zu sprechen? Ich wünsche mit Ihrer Frau Mutter zu sprechen. Haben Sie Geld, um diesen Ring zu kaufen? Hast du Zeit, mir meine Aufgabe zu verbessern? Hat dein Vater dir dieses Geld gegeben, um es so schlecht anzuwenden?

108.

Das Unglück, öön'-glück, the misfortune.

It is no subject for laughter (in order to laugh.) It is very difficult. I have had the pleasure to dance with Miss N. Mr. Nollet has had the kindness to lend me his horse. Do you wish to go out with me? I have no time to go to N. We have much to do to-day. My brother has six letters to copy. I have good news to communicate to you. Have the kindness to send me back my book. It is time to set out. Which dress do you wish to put on? Allow me to open the window, it is so warm. I am come to see, if you are well (wohl). I am very (much) indisposed; I have too much to do. You have the bad habit, to get up too late. A young man must get up earlier. My friend has had the misfortune to lose his parents. I come to bring you your boots. That is very well (gut). I had no mind to wait (any) longer.

109.

Jch werde geliebt, I am loved;	Jch wurde geliebt, I was loved;
du wirst geliebt,	du wurdest geliebt,
er wird geliebt,	er wurde geliebt,
wir werden geliebt,	wir wurden geliebt,
ihr werdet geliebt,	ihr wurdet geliebt,
sie werden geliebt.	sie wurden geliebt.

Belohnen, bai-lo'-nen, to reward; strafen, strå'-fen, to punish; achten, åch'-ten, to esteem; verachten, fer-åch'-ten, to despise; geschickt, gai-shickt', clever, skillful; unwissend, öön''-viss'-sent, ignorant; artig, åhr'-tich, pretty, agreeable, civil, well-behaved.

Obs. 1. In order to form the passive voice of a verb, its past participle is construed with the auxiliary verb werden throughout all the different moods and tenses. Thus:

Pres. Jch werde geliebt, I am loved.   *Imp.* Jch wurde geliebt, I was loved.

I. Fut. Jch werde geliebt werden, I shall be loved.   *II. Fut.* Jch werde geliebt worden sein, I shall have been loved.

Perf. Jch bin geliebt worden, I have been loved.   *Pluperf.* Jch war geliebt worden, I had been loved

Obs. 2. In the formation of the passive voice the abridged form w o r d e n is always used instead or e w o r d e n.

Jch werde von meinem Vater gelobt, wenn ich fleißig und artig bin. Du wirst von deinem Lehrer getadelt, weil du immer faul bist. Hein-rich wird gestraft, weil er unartig ist. Welcher Mann wird gelobt und welcher wird getadelt? Der geschickte Mann wird gelobt und der un-wissende getadelt. Welche Knaben werden belohnt und welche werden gestraft? Diejenigen, welche fleißig sind, werden belohnt und die, welche faul sind, gestraft. Wir werden von unsern Eltern geliebt; ihr werdet von den eurigen getadelt. Meine Brüder werden von Jedermann ge-achtet. Wir werden von unsern Feinden verachtet. Wird dieses Kind nie gestraft? Von wem werdet ihr gelobt? Deine Schwester wird von ihrer Mutter getadelt, weil sie nicht arbeitet. Jch wurde immer von meinem Lehrer geliebt und gelobt, weil ich fleißig und artig war. Heinrich wurde immer von seinem Vater gestraft, wenn er nicht ar-beitete.

110.

Ich bin geliebt worden, I have been loved;   wir sind geliebt worden, we have been loved;
du bist geliebt worden,   ihr seid geliebt worden,
er ist geliebt worden,   sie sind geliebt worden.

Töbten, tö'-ten, to kill; erfunden, err-foon'-den, invented; entbeckt, ent-deckt', discovered; Pulver, pool'-fer, gunpowder; mehre, mai'-rai, several.

Ich bin von meinem Vater gestraft worden, weil ich diese Briefe nicht abgeschrieben habe. Du bist von deinem Onkel belohnt worden, weil du seine Uhr gefunden hast. Heinrich ist für seine Mühe nicht belohnt worden. Diese Nachricht ist uns durch Herrn Moll mitgetheilt worden. Von wem ist diese Aufgabe verbessert worden? Wir sind von diesem Menschen mehrere Male beleidigt worden. Diese Herren sind gestern in der Gesellschaft sehr getadelt worden. Dieses Kind ist von seiner Mutter gewaschen worden. Es ist mir gesagt worden, daß Sie einen Bedienten suchten. Von wem sind diese Kinder geschickt worden? Diese Häuser sind gestern alle verkauft worden. Wir sind oft von unserm Lehrer gelobt worden, weil wir immer unsere Aufgaben machten. Gustav Adolph ist bei Lützen getödtet worden. Das Pulver ist von Berthold Schwarz erfunden worden. Amerika ist von Kolumbus entdeckt worden.

111.

Sich freuen, froi'-en, to rejoice; gefreut, gai-froit', rejoiced.

Ich freue mich, I rejoice;   Ich habe mich gefreut, I have rejoiced;
du freust dich,   du hast dich gefreut,
er freut sich,   er hat sich gefreut,
wir freuen uns,   wir haben uns gefreut,
ihr freuet euch,   ihr habt euch gefreut,
sie freuen sich.   sie haben sich gefreut.

Sich irren, irr'-ren, to be mistaken; sich befinden, bai-fin'-den, to be, to do; sich wundern, voon'-dern, to be astonished; sich ankleiden, ân''-kli'-den, to dress (one's self); sich unterhalten, öön'-ter-hâl''-ten, to be amused; banken, dânk'-en, to thank; zweifeln, tsvi'-feln, to doubt; wiedersehen, vee''-der-sey'-hen, to see again; selten, zel'-ten, seldom; auf, ouf, on, upon.

Guten Tag, lieber Heinrich. Ich freue mich, dich wiederzusehen. Wie geht es? Wie befindest du dich? Ich danke dir, ich befinde mich sehr wohl, seit ich auf dem Lande wohne. Was macht dein Bruder? Ist er wohl? Ja, er befindet sich sehr wohl. Was thust du, Ludwig? Ich kleide mich an. Kleidet ihr euch noch nicht an? Wir werden uns später ankleiden. Haben Sie sich schon gewaschen, Henriette? Ich habe mich noch nicht gewaschen, aber meine Schwester hat sich schon gewaschen. Ist das mein Bruder, der da mit dem Herrn N. kommt? Sie irren sich, es ist nicht Ihr Bruder. Ich glaube nicht, daß ich mich irre. Ich irre mich selten. Ich habe mich noch nie geirrt. Wir gehen diesen Abend nach N. Ich zweifle nicht, daß wir uns gut unterhalten werden. Wie haben Sie sich gestern in dem Concert unterhal-

4

ten? Sehr gut, Herr N. hat sehr gut gespielt. Ich wundere mich, daß Sie nicht da waren. Ich hatte noch Vieles zu thun; ich habe bis zehn Uhr gearbeitet.

112.

Art thou not yet dressed, Charles? I shall dress myself at present. Why hast thou not yet dressed thyself? I had still two exercises to do. I rejoice to see, that thou art so diligent. I love him, who rejoices when his friend is praised. I saw your brother yesterday. You are mistaken; my brother is no longer here. I am not mistaken, I have seen him with his friend Ferdinand. Why have you not washed yourself? I should have washed myself, if I had had any water. We were in the country yesterday; we have been very much amused. How does your sister do? She is very well, since she has been (is) with her uncle. And how have you been, since I saw you? I have been very well. I am astonished that you are not yet departed. I shall set out this evening.

113.

Es regnet, raich'-net, it rains;   es freut mich, I am glad, happy;
es schneit, shni't, it snows;   es thut mir leid, lite, I am sorry;
es hagelt, hâ'-ghelt, it hails;   es ist mir kalt, I am cold;
es blitzt, blitst, it lightens;   es ist mir warm, I am warm;
es bonnert, don'-nert, it thunders;   es hungert mich, höön'-ghert, I am hungry;
es friert, free'-ert, it freezes;   es durstet mich, döör'-stet, I am thirsty.

Befehlen, bai-fai'-len, to command; bleiben, bli'-ben, to stay; zu Mittag essen, mit'-tâhch, to dine; leben Sie wohl, vo'l, farewell, adieu.

Regnet es? Nein, es regnet nicht. Es regnete, als ich gekommen bin. Es hat die ganze Nacht geregnet. Es wird morgen gewiß reg= nen. Ich glaube, daß es schneit. Hat es geschneit? Wenn es schneite, würde es nicht regnen. Es wird diese Nacht frieren, denn es ist sehr kalt. Ich muß ausgehen, aber es hagelt, wie ich sehe. Mir ist sehr warm; es blitzt, sogleich wird es donnern. Wir wollen nach Haus ge= hen. Es freut mich, daß ich Sie finde; aber es thut mir leid, daß ich nicht mit Ihnen gehen kann. Mein Onkel ist gestern Abend angekom= men und wünscht, daß wir heute bei ihm zu Mittag essen. Haben Sie nichts zu trinken, mich durstet sehr. Wünschen Sie ein Glas Bier oder Wasser? Sie haben nur zu befehlen; hier ist, was Sie wünschen. Aber mich hungert auch; geben Sie mir ein Stück Schinken und ein wenig Brot. Sie haben da schöne Birnen und Pflaumen. Es gibt dieses Jahr viel Obst. Wollen Sie heute bei uns bleiben? Ich danke Ihnen, ich habe meinem Vetter versprochen, heute mit ihm nach S. zu gehen; er wird mich gewiß schon erwarten. Leben Sie wohl.

114.

Was für Wetter ist es? What kind of weather is it?

What sort of weather is it? It is bad weather; it is raining
(it rains). It did not rain when you came. It will rain the whole
day. It has been raining this morning. Does it snow? No, it does
not snow. It would snow, if it were colder. I believe, that it freezes.
The weather is finer to-day; it is warm. I am very warm. It has
lightened; it will thunder later. I am sorry that you are not come
sooner. Art thou hungry? Yes I am hungry and thirsty. I have
taken (made) a long walk. I shall drink a glass of wine, if you (will)
allow it. My sister will be happy to see you again. She has often
spoken of you to me. Will your nephew come also? I doubt whether
he will come (comes). He has too much to do.

115.

Wie viel Uhr ist es?	What o'clock is it?
es ist sechs Uhr,	it is six o'clock;
es ist halb sieben,	it is half past six;
es ist ein Viertel auf sieben,	it is a quarter past six.

Aufstehen, ouf'-stey-hen, to get up; schlafen gehen, shlä'-fen, to go to bed; ausruhen,
ouss''-roo'-hen, to repose; spazieren, spazieren gehen, spât-see'-ren, to go, to walk.

Um wie viel Uhr stehen Sie gewöhnlich auf? Ich stehe jeden Morgen um sechs Uhr auf und gehe um zehn Uhr schlafen. Sind Sie spazieren gewesen? Ja, ich habe eine Stunde in dem Walde spaziert. Ich
bin sehr müde, ich will ein wenig ausruhen. Wie viel Uhr ist es? Es
ist acht Uhr; es ist noch nicht halb neun. Um wie viel Uhr sind Sie
angekommen? Ich bin um ein Viertel auf sechs angekommen. Meine
Schwester ist um drei Viertel auf acht abgereist. Wie lange bleiben Sie,
hier? Ich werde nur zwei bis drei Tage bleiben. Um wie viel Uhr
essen wir zu Mittag? Ich glaube um zwölf Uhr oder um halb eins.
Um drei Uhr trinken wir Kaffee und um sieben Uhr essen wir zu Nacht.
Die Deutschen essen jeden Tag vier Mal und die Franzosen nur zwei
Mal. Ich finde, daß die Franzosen Recht haben. Der Mensch lebt
nicht, um zu essen und zu trinken.

116.

Zu Abend essen, to sup.

Zahlreich, tsåh!'-ri'ch, numerous; vor, fore, before; nach Hause, home.

Have the kindness to tell me what o'clock it is. It is not yet
eleven o'clock; it is half past ten. I must depart at twelve o'clock,
or at half past twelve. Have you already dined? No, I shall dine
with my cousin; we dine generally at two o'clock. At what o'clock
do you sup? I shall sup at nine o'clock. Have you a mind to walk
a little? If it does not rain, I shall walk a little with you. It is

fine weather; we will go to N., we shall find there a numerous party (Gefellſchaft). Are you already tired? I am very tired; it is too warm. If you allow (it) I will repose a little. Get up; it is time to go home. I must go to bed before ten o'clock, in order to get up ◑-morrow at five o'clock.

117.

Prepositions governing the:

Accusative.	*Dative.*
Für, fü'r, for;	auß, ouss, out of;
burch, döörch, through;	mit, mit, with;
ohne, oh'-nai, without;	nach, nâch, to, after;
gegen, ghey'-ghen, to, towards, against;	von, fon, from;

Dative and Accusative.

an, ân, at, of;	in, in, into;
auf, ouf, upon, on;	unter, öön'-ter, under.

Friebrich, Free'-drich, Frederick; der Martt, mârrkt, market; der Wille, vil'-lai, the will; der Keller, kel'-ler, cellar; die Kirche, kirr'-chai, church; die Küche, küch'-chai, kitchen; legen, lai'-ghen, to put, to lay; fißen, zit'-tsen, to sit; wohin, vo-hin', whither, where to; woher, vo-hair', whence, from where.

Obs. The prepositions an, auf, in, unter, govern the Accusative, when the verb of the phrase denotes a motion or a direction towards an object; and the Dative, when it does not express this motion.

Für wen ſind dieſe Bücher? Dieſes iſt für mich und jenes iſt für meine Schweſter. Wo iſt der junge Mann, für den Sie alle dieſe Sa= chen gekauft haben? Durch welche Straße müſſen wir gehen, um auf den Marft zu kommen? Durch die Friedrichsſtraße ober die Wilhelms= ſtraße? Gehen Sie ohne Regenschirm aus? Es wird ſogleich regnen. Was iſt das Leben ohne einen Freund? Ich kann ohne dich nicht leben. Du biſt gegen den Willen deines Vaters ausgegangen. Warum iſt dein Bruder immer gegen mich? Woher kommſt du? Ich komme vom Spaziergange, aus der Schule, aus der Kirche. Die Magd kommt aus dem Keller, aus dem Garten, aus der Küche. Mit wem ſeid ihr ausge= gangen? Mit dem Onkel, mit der Tante, mit ihnen. Nach dem Eſ= ſen gehen wir aus. Wann kommen Sie zurück? Kommen Sie vor ober nach uns zurück? Wir werden nach Ihnen zurückkommen. Wo iſt meine Schweſter? Sie iſt in der Kirche, in dem Garten, auf dem Marfte. Wohin geht deine Mutter? Sie geht in die Küche, in den Keller, auf den Marft. Wohin haſt du mein Buch gelegt? Ich habe es auf den Tiſch, unter den Stuhl gelegt. Wo iſt die kleine Luiſe? Sie ſitzt auf dem Stuhle, unter dem Tiſche, an der Thüre. Schreiben Sie an Ihren Vetter ober an Ihre Baſe? An wen denken Sie? Ich denke an die arme Frau, welche ich geſtern bei Ihnen geſehen habe.

118.

Der Schrant, shrânk, the press, closet; unbanfbâr; öön''-dânk'-bar, ungrateful.

This is for me, that is for you. He who is not for me, is against me. I cannot do this without him, without her, without you. I shall arrive before you; you will arrive after me. You are ungrateful towards us. I always think of you, but you never think of me. There is thy little sister; hast thou nothing for her? You do not love my brother, you are always against him. Where is your son? This fruit and these flowers are for him. Where have you been? We have been at (in the) church and at (in the) school. Where are you going? We are going into the garden, to (on the) market, into the kitchen. Where do these children come from? They come from the public walk (Spaziergang), from church, from the garden. Where have you put my stockings and shoes? I have put them on your chair, on the table, in the closet. Have you seen my brother? I have seen him at the public walk, in the garden, at the door. I write to my uncle and aunt. We often speak of him and of her.

119.

Im	instead of	in bem;		am	instead of	an bem;
ins	"	" in bas;		ans	"	" an bas;
zum	"	" zu bem;		vom	"	" von bem;
zur	"	" zu ber;		unterm	"	" unter bem.

Das Feuer, foi'-er, the fire; sich stellen, stel'-len, to place one's self, to stand; das Schreibzeug, shripe'-tsoich, the writing stand, writing materials; die Bleifeder, bli''-fai'-der, the lead pencil.

Obs. The quickness of the pronunciation has introduced the custom of contracting the definite article with certain prepositions.

Die Magd ist im Keller oder im Garten. Wir gehen diesen Abend ins Theater oder ins Concert. Schicken Sie den Bedienten zum Schuster oder zum Schneider? Gehen wir heute zur Tante oder bleiben wir zu Hause? Waren Sie gestern bei dem Minister? Kommen Sie zu mir oder zu meinem Bruder? Warum sitzen Sie immer beim Feuer? Ist Ihnen so kalt? Was haben Sie am Auge, am Fuße? Warum tragen Sie eine Feder am Hute? Stellen Sie sich an die Thüre oder ans Fenster. Haben Sie diese Blume vom Gärtner erhalten? Sie arbeiten vom Morgen bis zum Abend. Was machen Sie unterm Tische? Ich suche meine Bleifeder. Karl hat sie ins Schreibzeug gelegt.

120.

Her, hair, to this place, hither; hin, hin, thither, along.

Wovon, of what;		davon, of that, of it;
womit, with what;		damit, with that, with it;
wozu, for what;		dazu, for that, for it;
woran, at what;		daran, at that, at it;
worin, in what;		darin, in that, in it;
woburch, by what;		baburch, by that, by it.

Herab, hinab, down;
herauf, hinauf, up;
herein, hinein, in

Brauchen, brou'-chen, to use, vant, need; gesprochen, gai-sproch'-chen, spoken; gedacht, gai-dächt', thought; ging, ghink, went; fiel, feel, fell; das Clavier, klâ-veer', the piano.

Obs. 1) All these particles are formed of prepositions, combined with the adverbs wa, ba, her and hin. If, in the formation of these words, two vowels meet, an r is inserted, to avoid the hiatus. 2) Her denotes a motion towards the person speaking; hin a motion from the speaker.

Wovon sprechen Sie? Ist dies das Buch, wovon Sie sprechen? Womit haben Sie das gemacht? Ist das die Feder, womit Sie diesen Brief geschrieben haben? Wozu brauchen Sie das? Woran denken Sie denn? Ist das das Haus, worin Ihr Onkel wohnt, die Stadt, wodurch Sie gekommen sind? Hat man von meinem Unglück gesprochen? Ja, man hat davon gesprochen. Haben Sie an meine Sache gedacht? Nein, ich habe nicht daran gedacht. Sind Sie mit Ihrem neuen Klavier zufrieden? Nein, ich bin nicht zufrieden damit. Ist noch Wein in der Flasche? Nein, es ist keiner mehr darin. Wie viel Ellen müssen sie zu einem neuen Rocke haben? Ich muß drei und eine halbe Elle dazu haben. Kommen Sie herauf. Gehen Sie hinab, hinunter. Warum kommen Sie nicht herein? Warum gehen Sie nicht hinein? Der Knabe ging zu nah' ans Wasser und fiel hinein. Werden Sie diesen Abend ins Theater gehen? Wir werden nicht hingehen, aber Heinrich und Karl gehen hin.

121.

Bitten, bit'-ten, to beg, ask; der Krieg, kreech, the war; das Schauspiel, shou'-speel, the play; sogleich, zo-gli'ch', instantaneously, directly; Concert, con-tserrt', the concert.

Do you know of what I speak, of what I think? That is not the same street, through which we came (are come) this morning, the same house where we were yesterday. Do you speak of (the) war? Yes, we speak of it. Do you think of the concert? We do not think of it. Are you pleased with this ring? I am very (much) pleased with it. Why do you not come up? Tell your brother that I am coming down directly. Come in, my friends. I beg you to come in. Do you go to the play this evening? We shall not go there. Do you know, where this gentleman lives, where he goes to, and where he is? We do not know it.

122.

Das Tischchen, tish'-chen, the little table, die Taube, tou'-bai, the pigeon, dove; das Täubchen, toip'chen, the little dove; pflanzen, pflân'-tsen, to plant; eben, so eben, ai'-ben, just now, just.

Obs. Diminutives are formed by adding the syllables chen or lein, and softening the radical vowel. If the primitive word ends in e or en, the e or en is omitted.

Amalie hat ihr Hütchen verloren. Wir haben drei hübsche Bäumchen gepflanzt. Wem gehört dieses artige Gärtchen? Wie viel hast du für dieses Täubchen bezahlt? Wohin gehen diese Herrchen? Komm

Luischen, wir wollen zu der Tante gehen, sie hat ein neues Kätzchen und ein neues Hündchen. Ich habe eben ein Briefchen von meiner Schwester erhalten, worin sie mich bittet, ihr ein Messerchen und ein Löffelchen zu kaufen. Ich will recht artig sein, Mütterchen, wenn du mir ein neues Kleidchen kaufst. Trage dieses Tischchen in den Garten, Henriette, wir wollen ein Stündchen darin arbeiten. Welches Dörfchen sehe ich da unten im Walde? Welches Kind hat diese Schühchen verloren? Friedrich hat ein artiges Vögelchen vom Gärtner erhalten. Wem gehören alle diese Blümchen? Wo ist dein Schwesterchen, Johann?

123.

Nöthig (nö'-tich) haben, to want; sich schämen, shai'-men, to be ashamed of; pflegen, pflai'-ghen, to use, to be in the habit of; schläfrig, shlai'-frich, sleepy; Durst (döörrst) haben, to be thirsty; Spaziergang, spät-seer'-ghânk, walk; scheinen, shi'-nen, to shine, to appear; früh, frü, early; spät, spait, late; ich möchte, möch'-tai, I should like; geschwinde, gai-shwin'-dai, fast, quickly; Geduld, gai-döölt', patience; fürchten, fürrch'-ten, to fear, to be afraid.

Heinrich, hast du Lust einen Spaziergang mit mir zu machen? Ich habe keine Lust, jetzt auszugehen. Ich bin schläfrig. Schämst du dich nicht, so faul zu sein? Komm, wir wollen in den Garten meines Onkels gehen. Wie viel Uhr ist es? Es ist erst sechs Uhr, die Sonne scheint noch. Du hast Recht, es ist noch früh, ich will mit dir gehen. Ich pflege jeden Abend einen Spaziergang zu machen, ehe ich zu Bette gehe. Das ist eine gute Gewohnheit. Es ist mir aber sehr warm; wir gehen zu geschwinde. Ich habe großen Durst, ich möchte einmal trinken. Wenn man warm ist, muß man nicht trinken. Ich habe nöthig, ein wenig auszuruhen; ich bin so müde, daß ich nicht mehr fort kann. Du mußt einen Augenblick Geduld haben. Komm, ich fürchte zu spät nach Hause zu kommen.

124.

To have patience, Geduld haben; to be hard-hearted, hartherzig (hârrt''-herrt'-sich) sein; to have the head-ache, Kopfweh (kopf'-vey) haben; to take pains, sich bemühen, bai-mü'-hen; some pretext, ein Vorwand (*masc.*), fore'-vânt; the advice, der Rath, râht; the patient, der Kranke, krank'-ai; the idler, der Faulenzer, fou'-len-tser; the fault, der Fehler, fai'-ler; directly, sogleich, zo-gli'ch'.

How, you are still in bed? Are you not ashamed, to sleep so long? I should be ashamed to get up so late. I cannot get up today, I have the head-ache. You are a little idler. When you must go to school, you always look for some pretext. You are in the habit of going to bed early and getting up late. That is a bad habit. I beg you, to have patience (for) a moment. I shall get up directly. I have no mind, to wait (any) longer. I fear to come to church too late. You are very hard-hearted; you have no pity for a poor patient. You are not ill; you have no mind to go to school. You are right my friend; I shall take pains to get rid of this fault (biefen Fehler abzulegen) and to follow your good advice.

125.

Glauben, to believe.

I believe that it is already late. We do not believe it. Neither does my brother believe it. Do you believe it? I do not believe it. If I did believe it, you would laugh. I have never believed this. Who would have believed that? I should believe it, if you told me so (it me). It is an incredible thing. You would believe it indeed, if you saw it. These gentlemen do not believe it. How will you have me (that I should) believe it? Your brother believed every thing that was told him (all that one told him); he was too credulous. He would not believe it, if he knew you.

Also, auch, ouch; neither, auch nicht; you would laugh, Sie würden lachen (so würden Sie lachen); would have, hätte; incredible, unglaublich, öön'-gloup''-lich; indeed, wohl; if you saw, wenn Sie fähen; credulous, leichtgläubig, li'cht''-gloi'-bich; if he knew, wenn er kennte.

126.

Sagen, to say, to tell.

I have something to tell you. What have you to say to me? I tell you nothing. Tell (it) me only. I shall tell you another time. You will not tell my brother, what I have written to you. Do not tell him, that I am still in bed. What has he told you? Have I not told it you? You have not yet told (it) me. Do you wish (will you) me to (that I) tell it? One must not tell everything that one knows. He has told it me in a whisper. Your uncle told me yesterday, that he would sell his house. What do you say to that? I would tell you with pleasure, if I knew it. If I said otherwise, I should lie.

Knows, weiß; in a whisper, ins Ohr, ore; if I knew, wenn ich wüßte; otherwise, anders, än'-ders; lie, lügen, lü'-ghen.

127.

Wünschen, to wish; hoffen, hof'-fen, to hope.

I wish, that your enterprise may succeed. We often wish (for) things, which are hurtful to us. I should wish to be able to serve you. I hope, that our friend will obtain the situation that he wishes (to get). She did hope to win her law-suit, but she was mistaken. My cousin has nothing more to hope. We hope everything of Providence. My sister hopes, that you will do what you have promised her. Never wish (for) what you cannot have. What do you wish?

(For) what do you hope? I believe that my father will arrive to-day. We must hope it. These gentlemen wish that we should depart. Does your sister wish to go with us?

May succeed, gelinge; hurtful, ſchädlich, shait'-lich; to serve, dienen (dee'-nen), nützlich ſein; obtain, erhalten; situation, die Stelle, stel'-lai; win, gewinnen, gai-vin'-nen; law-suit, der Prozeß, pro-tsees'; Providence, die Vorſehung, fore''-zey'-hoönk; for what, worauf, vo-rouf'.

128.

Schreiben, to write;   ich ſchrieb, shreep, I wrote;   geſchrieben, written;
leſen, to read;   ich las, I read;   geleſen, read.

I am writing a letter to my brother. My mother will write to him to-morrow. You wrote better formerly. What have you written to him? Have you not yet written to him, that our friend Henry is dead? Write that to him. If I had a good pen, I should write also. You write too fast; write more slowly. Show me what you have written. You must write once more. What do you read? I read an amusing book. What didst thou read yesterday, when thou wast with thy uncle? I read the fables of Gellert, which are very well written. We should read oftener if we had more time. How must we (one) read this word? Remember well, what you have read. Would you like (will you) me to (that I should) read this letter to you? I should like to know how to read like you.

Formerly, früher, frü'-her, ſonſt, zonst; fast, ſchnell, shnell; slowly, langſam, lânk'-zâhm; more slowly, langſamer; show, zeigen, tsi'-ghen; once more, noch einmal, ine'-mâhl; amusing, unterhaltend, ŏŏn'-ter-hâl''-tent; fable, die Fabel, fâ'-bel; remember, behalten, bai-hâl'-ten; I should like to know how, ich möchte können; like, wie, vee.

129.

Sehen, to see;   ich ſah, I saw;   geſehen, seen;
kennen, to know;   ich kannte, I knew;   gekannt, known.

What do I see? Do you not see it? I see nothing. But do look. It is well worth the trouble, to see it. I saw your cousin yesterday. Have you not seen him? Do you see how I do this? Your cousin does not see me. If I saw my friend, I should tell him, that you are here. Would you like (will you) me to (that I) bring (a) light; or can you see still? I have seen Mr. N. to-day. Does he know me? I believe that he knows you. He has greeted me. Have you also known my uncle? Have you not told me, that you knew him? I should know him again, if I saw him. Your brother has recognized me by my voice. These children do not know me (any) more.

Do look, ſehen Sie doch einmal; well worth the trouble, wohl der Mühe werth (vairt); to greet, grüßen, grü'-sen; to know again, to recognize, wieder erkennen, vee'-der er-ken'-nen; by the voice, an der Stimme, stim'-mai.

4*

130.

Gehen, to go; ich ging, I went; gegangen, gone;
weggehen, vech″-ghey′-hen, to go away; ausgehen, ouss″-ghey′-hen, to go out.

Where are you going? I am going to my aunt, and my brother goes to school. Where did you go this morning with your cousin? We went to church. I should willingly go to walk, if you would go with me. I shall go with you, but do not go so fast. Where is your sister? She is gone to see her uncle. We should have gone together if I had had time. Shall you not go to N. to-morrow? My father does not wish (will not) me to (that I should) go there. I go away. Do you go away already? Henry does not yet go away. William is already gone away. Go away. I must go away. I believe that your friends are gone away already. At what o'clock do you go out? I go out every morning at seven o'clock. And at what o'clock dost thou go out? I went out yesterday at six o'clock. Is your brother already gone out? To-morrow I shall go out early. I must go out at half past one. My mother did not wish (would not) that I should go out (went out).

To go to walk, spazieren gehen; to go to see any one, zu Jemandem gehen.

131.

Kommen, to come; ich kam, I came; gekommen, come;
zurückkommen, to come back; ankommen, to arrive.

Whence do you come so late? We come out of the garden. Eliza does not come to-day; she is gone into the country with her father. Come to see me this afternoon. It is possible that I may come. I should wish that you came early. Formerly you came every day. I should come oftener if I had not so much to do. My brother is not yet come back. He will come back this evening. My uncle does not come back (any) more. We saw your uncle, when we came back from the country. At what o'clock does the post arrive? I believe it arrives at three o'clock. Yesterday it came very late. Formerly it arrived at two o'clock. My sisters will arrive to-day from Liege.

Eliza, Elise, ai-lee′-zai; to come to see, besuchen, bai-zoo′-chen; afternoon, Nachmittag, nách″-mit′-táhch; possible, möglich, mö'ch′-lich; the post, mail, die Post, pöst (poss't); Liege, Lüttich, Lüt′-tich.

132.

Trinken, to drink; ich trank, I drank; getrunken, drunk;
austrinken, to finish (a glass, a cup etc.)
essen, to eat; ich aß, I ate; gegessen, eaten.

Have you nothing to drink? I drink no wine. We drink only water, and my brother drinks beer. You do not drink. I have the honor to drink your health. When I was young, I drank nothing but (only) milk. This gentleman has drunk a little too much. He does not eat much, but he drinks much. Who has drunk out of my glass? I will drink no more. We will drink another glass. The wine which we drank yesterday was so good, that every one drank a bottle. Finish your glass. You have not yet finished your glass. Drink again. Have you no appetite? Eat a little ham. I have eaten enough, I have no more appetite. You will eat another piece of meat. This child eats the whole day. We ate some days ago (some) delicious fish. At what o'clock do you dine? I dine generally at two o'clock, but to-day I dine at four o'clock. After dinner I drink a cup of coffee and then I go out to walk.

To your health, auf Ihre Gesundheit, gai-zöönt′-hite; the honor, die Ehre, ey′-rai; another glass, noch ein Glas; every one, Jeder, yey′-der; again, noch einmal; the appetite, der Appetit, âp-pai-teet′; some days ago, vor einigen Tagen; delicious fish, köstliche Fische, köst′-lich-chai fish′-shai; the dinner, das Mittagessen, mit′′-tâhchs-ess′-sen; then, dann, dân.

133.

| Können, to be able, to know; | ich konnte, I could; | gekonnt, been able; |
| wissen, to know; | ich wußte, I knew; | gewußt, known. |

Can you tell me, what o'clock it is? I cannot tell (it) you, I have not (got) my watch with me. If I had it with me, I could tell you exactly. I shall not be able to go out to-day; my father is ill. My brother will not be able to come. I should wish however that he could come. I should be able to lend you this book, if it belonged to me. Lewis can carry this letter to the post-office. I could not go out yesterday. My friend could not answer your letter, because he had too much to do. Do you know when my father will come back? I do not know. Does your sister know it? We know all, that we must die. Do you know (how) to dance? I have known it, but I do not know it (any) more. My father knew several languages. Henry can speak German. These two boys know neither how to read nor how to write. The men do not know (how) to employ their time. I did not know that your brother was departed. I shall soon know, who has done that. How can you suppose (will you) that I should know this? I should wish that you knew it. (I would etc.)

Exactly, genau, gai-nou′; however, jedoch, yai-doch′; I should wish, ich wollte; to belong, gehören, gai-hö′-ren; answer, antworten (ânt′′-vorr′-ten) auf (Acc.); because, weil, vile; to speak German, deutsch (doitsh) sprechen.

134.

| Thun, to do; | ich that, I did; | gethan, done; |
| nehmen, to take; | ich nahm, I took; | genommen, taken. |

What are you doing? I do, what you have ordered me (to do).
What where you doing, when I came in? I was lighting the
fire. What will you do this evening? I shall do nothing this
evening. Your brother does nothing but run. These children do
nothing but drink and eat. When one has done one's duty, one
has nothing to reproach one's self (with). You have done a good
action. Why are you in bad spirits? What have they done to
you? One must do the will of God. You will write to him; in
your place I should not do it. I shall do my best to satisfy him.
I take this for myself. How many books do you take? Your
brother always takes my pen. Will you take my place? Take what
you wish. Take this child by the hand. Who has taken my copy-
book? Your cousin took my cane yesterday. I shall take one of
these apples, if you allow (it). I have taken the liberty to write
to him. We took some chairs and we sat down. If I took these
books, my father would scold me.

To order, befehlen; to come in, hereinkommen; to light, anzünden, ån''-tsün'-den;
nothing but, nichts als; one's duty, seine Pflicht, pflicht; to reproach one's self, sich
vorwerfen, fore''-verr'-fen; action, die Handlung, die That, hånd'-lóŏnk, tåht; in
bad spirits, übler Laune, ü'-bler lou'-nai; in your place, an Ihrer Stelle; to do one's
best, sein Möglichstes thun; to satisfy, befriedigen, bai-free'-dig-en; myself, mich;
place, Platz, plåts; by the hand, bei der Hand; liberty, die Freiheit, fri'-hite; to
sit down, sich setzen, zet'-tsen; to scold any one, mit Jemandem schmälen, shmai'-len;
the copy-book, das Schreibebuch, shri''-bai-booch'.

135.

Schlafen, to sleep;   ich schlief, shleef, I slept;   geschlafen, slept;
brechen, brech'-chen, zerbrechen, to break; ich brach, I broke;   gebrochen, broken.

We sleep too much; you sleep less than we. I sleep generally
(for) seven hours. Formerly I slept longer. My brother slept yesterday till eight o'clock; but to morrow he will not sleep so long,
because he must depart for Cologne at four o'clock. Our mother does
not allow us to sleep longer than till six o'clock. I sleep soundly.
You were very uneasy in your sleep last night. This child sleeps
very peaceably. We have no knife to cut our bread; therefore we
break it. You will break this stick, if you bend it so. I do not
believe that it (will) break. I should not like it to (that it did)
break. This boy has broken a pane. He broke two last week. This
servant is very heedless; she breaks something every day. Yesterday she broke two glasses, and on Sunday half a dozen cups and
saucers.

Less, weniger, vai'-nig-er; soundly, sehr fest, fest; to be uneasy in one's sleep,
unruhig (ŏŏn''-roo'-hich) schlafen; last, vorig, fo'-rich; peaceably, sanft, zånft; to cut,
schneiden, shni'-den; therefore, deshalb, dess'-hålp; to bend, beugen, boi'-ghen;

I should not like, i♦ mö♦te ni♦t; pane, bie S♦eibe, ahi'-bai; heedless, unbeba♦tfam,
ön''-bai-dâ♦t'-zâhm; on Sunday, am Sonntag, zon'-tâh♦; cups and saucers,
Taffen, tâss'-sen.

136.

Rathen, râ'-ten, to advise; i♦ rieth, reet, I advised; gerathen, gai-râ'-ten, advised;
bringen, to bring; i♦ bra♦te, I brought; gebra♦t, brought;
empfehlen, emp-fai'-len, to recommend; i♦ empfahl, I recommended; empfohlen, recommended.

I do not know what to resolve; what do you advise me to do?
One advises me this, the other that. They advised me yesterday,
to give up a part of my rights. I should like you to (that you advised) me; in you I have the greatest confidence. Because you wish
me to (that I) advise you, I tell you that the most unprofitable
accommodation is better than the most favorable law-suit. I shall
bring you the fruits which you desire (to have). I believe they have
brought them to me already. They brought me yesterday some letters from Berlin. When you come back, bring your sister with (you).
Mr. N. will bring his son with (him) to-morrow. They brought their
aunt with (them) from Vienna. I should wish you to bring (that you
brought) the young man with (you) of whom you have spoken. He
recommends his son to me. You recommended your business to him.
I have recommended him to watch over him.

Si♦ entf♦ließen, ent-ahlee'-sen, to resolve; what to resolve, wozu i♦ mi♦ ent-
f♦ließen foll; one, they, man; even, fogar, zo-gâhr'; to give up, abtreten, âp''-trai'-
ten; I should like, i♦ wollte; in you, zu Ihnen; the greatest confidence, bas meifte
Zutrauen, mi'-stai tsoo''-trou'-en; meager, unprofitable, mager, mâ'-gher; accommodation, compromise, ber Verglei♦, ferr-gli'♦'; the most unprofitable accommodation etc., ein magerer Verglei♦ ift beffer, als ein fetter Prozeß; to desire, wünf♦en;
to watch, wa♦en, vâ♦'-♦en; over, über, ü'-ber.

EXERCISES FOR READING AND TRANSLATING.

1. Der kleine Hund.

Ein Fräulein, mit Namen Karoline, ging einft an dem Ufer eines
Fluffes fpazieren. Sie begegnete hier einigen böfen Knaben, die ein
Hündchen ertränken wollten; fie hatte Mitleid mit dem armen Thiere,
kaufte es und nahm es mit fi♦ auf das Schloß.

Das Hündchen hatte bald mit feiner neuen Gebieterin Bekanntf♦aft
gema♦t und verließ fie keinen Augenblick mehr. Eines Abends, als fie
fi♦ zu Bette legen wollte, fing das Hündchen plötzlich an zu bellen. Karoline nahm das Licht, fah unter das Bett und erblickte einen Menf♦en
von für♦terli♦em Ausfehen, der fi♦ hier verborgen hatte. Es war
ein Dieb.

Karoline rief um Hülfe und alle Bewohner des Schlosses eilten auf
ihr Geschrei herbei. Sie ergriffen den Räuber und überlieferten ihn der
Gerechtigkeit. Er gestand in seinem Verhöre, daß es seine Absicht ge=
wesen wäre, das Fräulein zu ermorden, und das Schloß zu plündern.

Karoline dankte dem Himmel, daß er sie so glücklich gerettet habe, und
sagte: Niemand hätte geglaubt, daß das arme Thierchen, dem ich das
Leben gerettet habe, mir auch das meinige retten würde.

Der Name, nä'-mai, the name; mit Namen Karoline, whose name was Caroline;
das Ufer, öö'-fer, the bank, the shore; der Fluß, flööss, the river; ging spazieren, took
a walk; ertränken, err-trenk'-en, to drown; das Mitleid, mit'-lite, compassion, pity.

Bald, bàl't, soon; die Gebieterin, gai-bee'-tai-rin, mistress; die Bekanntschaft, bai-
kânt'-shâft, acquaintance; verlassen, ferr-lâss'-sen, to leave; verließ, fer-leess', left;
eines Abends, once of an evening: das Bett, bet, the bed; fing ... an, commenced;
bellen, bel'-len, to bark; plötzlich, plöts'-lich, suddenly, das Licht, licht, the light,
candle; erblicken, er-blick'-ken, to perceive; fürchterlich, fürch'-ter-lich, terrible; das
Aussehen, ouss''-zey'-hen, appearance, aspect; verborgen, fer-borr'-ghen, concealed;
der Dieb, deep, the thief.

Rufen, röö'-fen, to call; rief, reef, called; die Hülfe, hül'-fai, the help; der Bewohner, bai-vo'-ner, inhabitant, occupant; eilen, i'-len, to hurry; herbei, her-bi', hither;
das Geschrei, gai-shri', cry, shriek; der Räuber, roi'-ber, robber; ergreifen, er-gri'-
fen, to seize; sie ergriffen, they seized; überliefern, ü'-ber-lee''-fern, to deliver, to
hand over; die Gerechtigkeit, gai-rech'-tich-kite, justice, court of justice; gestehen, gai-
stey'-hen, to confess; gestand, confessed; das Verhör, fer-hö'r', trial; die Absicht,
âp'-zicht, design; gewesen wäre, (Subj. mood) had been; ermorden, er-morr'-den, to
murder; plündern, plün'-dern, to plunder, pillage.

Der Himmel, him'-mel, heaven; retten, ret'-ten, to save, preserve; das Leben, life.

2. Die guten Nachbarn.

Der kleine Knabe eines Müllers näherte sich zu sehr dem Bache und
fiel hinein. Der Schmid, welcher jenseit des Baches wohnte, sah es,
sprang in das Wasser, zog das Kind heraus und brachte es dem Vater.

Ein Jahr darauf brach während der Nacht Feuer in der Schmiede aus.
Das Haus stand ganz in Flammen, ehe der Schmid es merkte. Er ret=
tete sich mit Frau und Kindern. Nur sein kleinstes Töchterchen hatte
man im ersten Schrecken vergessen.

Das Kind fing in dem brennenden Hause an zu schreien; allein kein
Mensch wollte sich hinein wagen. Da kam plötzlich der Müller, sprang
in die Flammen, brachte das Kind glücklich heraus, gab es dem Schmid
in die Arme und sagte:

Gott sei gelobt, daß er mir Gelegenheit gab, Euch meine Dankbarkeit
zu beweisen. Ihr habt meinen Sohn aus dem Wasser gezogen und ich
habe mit Gottes Hülfe Eure Tochter aus dem Feuer errettet.

Der Müller, mül'-ler, miller; sich nähern, nai'-hern, to approach; der Bach, bâch,
the brook; fallen, fâl'-len, to fall; fiel, feel, fell; der Schmid, shmeet, black-smith;
jenseit (with Genit.), yen'-zite, on the other side of; springen, to spring, leap; ziehen,
tsee'-hen, to drag, to pull; zog, tso'ch, ... heraus (Imperf.), pulled out.

Die Schmiede, shmee'-dai, smith-shop; stehen, stey'-hen, to stand; stand, stood;

die Flamme, flâm'-mai, the flame; ehe, ey'-hai, before; merken, merr'-ken, to notice; vergessen, fer-gess'-sen, to forget; der Schrecken, shreck'-ken, terror, fright.
Brennend, burning; schreien, shri'-en, to scream; allein, âl-line', but; wagen, vâ'-ghen, to venture; der Arm, the arm.
Gott sei gelobt, God be praised; die Gelegenheit, gai-lai'-ghen-hite, opportunity; die Dankbarkeit, dânk'-bâhr-kite, gratitude; beweisen, bai-vi'-zen, prove, show.

3. Das zerbrochene Hufeisen. [1]

Ein Bauer ging mit seinem Sohne, dem kleinen Thomas, in die Stadt. Sieh, sagte er unterwegs zu ihm, da liegt ein Stück von einem Hufeisen an der Erde, hebe es auf und stecke es in die Tasche. Bah, versetzte Thomas, das ist nicht der Mühe werth, daß man sich dafür bückt. Der Vater erwiderte nichts, nahm das Eisen und steckte es in seine Tasche. Im nächsten Dorfe verkaufte er es dem Schmide für drei Heller und kaufte dafür Kirschen.

Hierauf setzten sie ihren Weg fort. Die Sonne war brennend heiß. Man sah weit und breit weder Haus, noch Wald, noch Quelle. Thomas verging vor Durst und konnte seinem Vater nur mit Mühe folgen.

Da ließ dieser, wie durch Zufall, eine Kirsche fallen. Thomas hob sie so gierig auf, als wäre es Gold, und steckte sie schnell in den Mund. Einige Schritte weiter ließ der Vater eine zweite Kirsche fallen, welche Thomas mit derselben Gierigkeit ergriff. Dies dauerte fort, bis er sie alle aufgehoben hatte.

Als er die letzte verzehrt hatte, wandte der Vater sich zu ihm hin und sagte: Sieh, wenn du dich ein einziges Mal hättest bücken wollen, um das Hufeisen aufzuheben, so würdest du nicht nöthig gehabt haben, es hundert Mal für die Kirschen zu thun.

Das Hufeisen, hoof''-i'-zen, the horse-shoe; zerbrochen, tser-broch'-chen, broken; der Bauer, bou'-er, farmer, peasant; unterwegs, öön''-ter-vaichss'', on the way; liegen, lee'-ghen, to lie; auf der Erde, on the ground; aufheben, ouf''-hai'-ben, to pick up; stecken, steck'-ken, to stick, to put; die Tasche, täsh'-shai, pocket; bah, pshaw; versetzen, fer-zet'-sen, to reply; bücken, bück'-ken, to stoop; erwiedern, er-vee'-dern, to answer; der Heller, penny.
Der Weg, vaich, the road, journey; fortsetzen, fort''-zet'-sen, to continue; heiß, hice, hot; weit und breit, vite ... brite, far and wide; weder ... noch, neither ... nor; die Quelle, quel'-lai, spring; verging, perished; folgen, fol'-ghen, to follow.
Lassen, lâss'-sen, to let; ließ fallen, let fall; wie durch Zufall, as if by accident; hob ... auf, picked up; gierig, ghee'-rich, eagerly; der Schritt, shritt, step; die Gierigkeit, ghee'-rich-kite, eagerness; fortdauern, forrt''-dou'-ern, to continue.
Verzehren, fer-tsai'-ren, to consume, to eat; wandte sich hin, turned; wenden, ven'-den, to turn; hundert Mal, höön'-dert mâhl, a hundred times.

4. Der verborgene Schatz. [1]

Kurz vor seinem Tode sagte ein Bauer zu seinen drei Söhnen: Liebe Kinder, ich kann euch nichts hinterlassen, als diese Hütte und den Weinberg, der daran stößt. Allein in diesem Weinberge liegt ein Schatz verborgen. Grabet fleißig nach, so werdet ihr ihn finden.

Nach dem Tode des Vaters gruben die Söhne den ganzen Weinberg mit dem größten Fleiße um, aber sie fanden weder Gold noch Silber. Da sie aber den Boden noch nie mit so viel Sorgfalt bearbeitet hatten, so brachte er eine solche Menge Trauben hervor, daß sie darüber erstaunten.

Jetzt erriethen die Söhne, was ihr Vater mit dem Schatze gemeint hatte, und sie schrieben an die Thür des Weinberges mit großen Buchstaben: Arbeitsamkeit ist der größte Schatz des Menschen.

Der Schatz, shâts, the treasure; verborgen, fer-borr'-ghen, hidden; kurz, koorts, shortly; hinterlassen, hin'-ter-lâss''-sen, to leave, bequeath; die Hütte, hüt'-tai, cottage, hut; der Weinberg, vine'-berrch, vine-yard; daran stoßen, sto'-sen, to border on, to adjoin; graben, grâ'-ben, to dig.

Der Tod, tote, death; gruben, dug; der Boden, bo'-den, the soil; bearbeiten, bai-ârr'-biten, to work; die Menge, meng'-ai, multitude, number, amount; die Traube, trou'-bai, the grape; hervorbringen, to bring forth; erstaunen, er-stou'-nen, to astonish, to be astonished.

Errathen, er-râ'-ten, to guess; erriethen (Imperf.); meinen, mi'-nen, to mean, intend; der Buchstabe, booch''-stâ'-bai, the letter; die Arbeitsamkeit, ârr'-bite-zähm-kite, industry.

5. Die Eiche und die Weide.

Nach einer sehr stürmischen Nacht ging ein Vater mit seinem Sohne auf das Feld, um zu sehen, welchen Schaden der Sturm verursacht habe. Sieh doch, rief der Knabe, da liegt die große, starke Eiche auf dem Boden hingestreckt, während die schwache Weide am Bache noch aufrecht dasteht. Ich hätte geglaubt, der Sturmwind würde leichter die Weide, als die Eiche niedergerissen haben.

Mein Sohn, sagte der Vater, die stolze Eiche, die sich nicht biegen kann, mußte brechen; allein die geschmeidige Weide hat dem Sturmwinde nachgegeben und ist daher verschont geblieben.

Stürmisch, stürr'-mish, stormy; das Feld, felt, the field; der Schaden, shâ'-den, injury, damage; der Sturm, stöörm, storm; verursachen, fer-oor''-zâch'-chen, to cause; hingestreckt, hin''-gai-streckt', stretched along; schwach, shwâch, weak; aufrecht, ouf'-recht, erect; niederreißen, nee''-der-ri'-sen, to tear down. Stolz, stölts, proud; biegen, bee'-ghen, to bend; geschmeidig, gai-shmi'-dich, pliant, supple; verschont, fer-sho'nt', spared, unharmed.

6. Der dankbare Löwe.

Ein armer Sklave, der aus dem Hause seines Herrn entflohen war, wurde zum Tode verurtheilt. Man führte ihn auf einen großen Platz, welcher mit Mauern umgeben war, und ließ einen furchtbaren Löwen auf ihn los. Tausende von Menschen waren Zeugen dieses Schauspiels.

Der Löwe sprang grimmig auf den armen Menschen zu; allein plötzlich blieb er stehen, wedelte mit dem Schweife, hüpfte voll Freude um ihn herum und leďte ihm freundlich die Hände. Jedermann verwunderte sich und fragte den Sklaven, wie das komme.

Der Sklave erzählte: Als ich meinem Herrn entlaufen war, verbarg ich mich in eine Höhle mitten in der Wüste. Da kam auf einmal dieser Löwe herein, winselte und zeigte mir seine Tatze, in der ein großer Dorn stak. Ich zog ihm den Dorn heraus und von der Zeit an versah mich der Löwe mit Wildpret und wir lebten in der Höhle friedlich zusammen. Bei der letzten Jagd wurden wir gefangen und von einander getrennt. Nun freut sich das gute Thier, mich wieder gefunden zu haben.

Alles Volk war über die Dankbarkeit dieses wilden Thieres entzückt und bat laut um Gnade für den Sklaven und den Löwen. Der Sklave wurde frei gelassen und reichlich beschenkt. Der Löwe folgte ihm wie ein Hündchen und blieb stets bei ihm, ohne Jemand ein Leid zu thun.

Dankbar, grateful; der Sclave, sklä'-fai, the slave; verurtheilen, fer-öör'-ti-len, to sentence; führen, fü'-ren, to lead; die Mauer, mou'-er, wall; umgeben, ööm-gai'-ben, to surround; furchtbar, föörcht'-bähr, formidable; ließ ... los, let loose; der Zeuge, tsoi'-gai, the witness.

Grimmig, grim'-mich, enraged; wedeln, vai'-deln, wag; der Schweif, shwife, tail; hüpfen, hüp'-fen, to leap, jump; die Freude, froi'-dai, pleasure; freundlich, froint'-lich, pleasantly; lecken, leck'-ken, to lick; fragen, frä'-ghen.

Die Höhle, hö'-lai, cave, cavern; mitten, in the midst of; die Wüste, vü'-stai, the desert; winseln, vin'-zeln, to moan, wail; die Tatze, tät'-tsai, the paw; stak, stähk, stuck; friedlich, freet'-lich, peaceably; die Jagd, yächt, the chase; fangen, fäng'-en, to capture; trennen, tren'-nen, to separate.

Wild, vilt, wild; entzückt, ent-tsückt', charmed, highly pleased; bitten, bit'-ten, to pray; laut, lout, loud; die Gnade, g'nä'-dai, grace, pardon; freilassen, to let loose, to set at liberty; reichlich, ri'ch'-lich, richly; beschenken, bai-shenk'-en, to present with; der Sclave .... beschenkt, the slave was set at liberty and presented with numerous gifts; stets, steyts, always; das Leid, lite, harm; Jemandem etwas zu Leid thun, to injure somebody.

5

66

COLLECTION OF WORDS.

1. Die Stadt (town).

Die Stadt, stât, the town;
die Vorstadt, fore'-stât, the suburb;
das Thor, tore, the gate;
der Platz, plâts, the square;
der Markt, mârrkt, the market-place;
die Straße, strâ'-sai, the street;
das Pflaster, pflâss'-ter, the pavement;
das Haus, house, the house;
das Gebäude, gai-boi'-dai, the building;
die Kirche, kirr'-chai, the church;
der Thurm, töörm, the tower, spire;
die Domkirche, dome''-kirr'-chai, the cathedral;
die Post, pöst, the post-office;

das Zollhaus, tsol'-house, the custom house;
das Theater, tai-â'-ter, the theatre;
die Börse, bör'-zai, the exchange;
das Spital, spee-tâhl', the hospital;
das Wirthshaus, virrts'-house, the inn;
das Kaffeehaus, kâf-fey''-house', the coffeehouse;
der Palast, pâ-lâst', the palace;
die Mauer, mou'-er, the wall;
die Festung, fess'-töönk, the fortress;
der Hafen, hâ'-fen, the harbor;
die Umgegend, ööm''-ghey'-ghent, the environs.

2. Das Haus (house).

Das Haus, house, the house;
die Thür, tü'r, the door;
das Schloß, shloss, the lock;
der Schlüssel, shlüss'-sel, the key;
die Klingel, kling'-el, the bell;
die Treppe, trep'-pai, the staircase;
eine Stufe, stoo'-fai, a step;
ein Zimmer, tsim'-mer, a room;
der Saal, zâhl, the saloon;
das Fenster, fen'-ster, the window;
die Laden, lâ'-den, the shutters;
die Decke, deck'-kai, the ceiling;

der Fußboden, fooss''-bo'-den, the floor;
die Wand, vânt, the wall;
der Kamin, kâ-meen', the chimney;
die Küche, küch'-chai, the kitchen;
der Keller, kel'-ler, the cellar;
der Speicher, spi'-cher, the ware-house;
das Dach, dâch, the roof;
der Hof, ho'f, the court-yard;
der Garten, gâr'-ten, the garden;
der Stall, stâl, the stable;
der Boden, bo'-den, garret, loft;
der Brunnen, bröön'-nen, the well.

3. Hausgeräthe (furniture).

Der Tisch, tish, the table;
der Stuhl, stool, the chair;
der Spiegel, spee'-ghel, the looking-glass;
der Schrank, shrânk, the wardrobe;
die Kommode, com-mo'-dai, the chest of drawers;
das Kanapee, câ'-nâ-pai, the couch;
das Gemälde, gai-mail'-dai, the picture;
die Standuhr, stânt'-oor, the clock;
das Bett, bet, the bed;
die Matratze, mâ-trât'-tsai, the mattress;
die Decke, deck'-kai, the coverlet;
der Ofen, o'-fen, the stove;
der Leuchter, loich'-ter, the candlestick;
der Löffel, löf'-fel, the spoon;

die Gabel, gâ'-bel, the fork;
das Messer, mess'-ser, the knife;
die Tasse, tâss'-sai, the cup and saucer;
das Tischtuch, tish'-tooch, the table-cloth;
das Tellertuch, tel''-ler-tooch', the napkin;
das Handtuch, hânt'-tooch, the towel;
die Lichtscheere, licht''-shai'-rai, the snuffers;
der Teller, tel'-ler, the plate;
das Kissen, kiss'-sen, the pillow;
das Betttuch, bet'-tooch, the sheet;
die Vorhänge, fore''-heng'-ai, the curtains;
das Glas, glâhss, the glass;
die Flasche, flâsh'-shai, the bottle;
der Korb, korp, the basket.

4. Gewerbe (professions).

Das Handwerk, hânt'-verrk, the profession;
der Handwerker, hânt''-verr'-ker, the artisan, mechanic;
der Metzger, mets'-gher, the butcher;
der Bäcker, beck'-ker, the baker;
der Müller, mül'-ler, the miller;
der Hutmacher, hoot''-mâch'-cher, the hatter;
der Schneider, shni'-der, the tailor;
der Schuster, shoo'-ster, the shoemaker;
der Barbier, bârr-beer', the barber;
der Schreiner, shri'-ner, the joiner;
der Zimmermann, tsim''-mer-mân', the carpenter;

der Glaser, glâ'-zer, the glazier;
der Schlosser, shloss'-ser, the lock-smith;
der Schmid, shmeet, the smith;
der Hufschmid, hoof'-shmeet, the farrier;
der Sattler, zât'-ler, the saddler;
der Böttcher, böt'-cher, the cooper;
der Gerber, gherr'-ber, the tanner;
der Kaufmann, kouf'-mân, the merchant;
der Buchhändler, booch''-hend'-ler, the bookseller;
der Buchbinder, booch''-bin'-der, the bookbinder;
der Maurer, mou'-rer, the mason;
die Näherin, nai'-tai-rin, the seamstress;
die Wäscherin, vesh'-shai-rin, the laundress.

5. Lebensmittel (victuals).

Das Brot, brote, the bread;
das Mehl, mail, the meal, flour;
das Fleisch, fli'sh, the meat;
der Braten, brâ'-ten, the roast-meat;
Kalbfleisch, kâlp'-fli'sh, veal;
Rindfleisch, rint'-fli'sh, beef;
Hammelfleisch, hâm''-mel-fli'sh', mutton;
der Fisch, fish, the fish;
das Ei, eye (I), the egg;
der Salat, zâl-lâ't', the salad;
der Senf, zenf, the mustard;
das Salz, zâlts, the salt;
das Oel, ö'l, the oil;
der Essig, ess'-sich, the vinegar;
Schweinefleisch, shwi''-nai-fli'sh', pork;
der Schinken, shink'-en, the ham;
das Gemüse, gai-mü'-zai, the vegetable;
die Suppe, zöep'-pai, the soup;

der Kohl, kole, the cabbage;
die Kartoffel, kâr-tof'-fel, the potatoe;
die Erbse, errp'-zai, the pea;
die Bohne, bo'-nai, the bean;
der Kuchen, koo'-chen, the cake;
das Obst, o'pst, the fruit;
der Pfeffer, pfef'-fer, the pepper;
die Butter, böot'-ter, the butter;
der Käse, kai'-zai, the cheese;
die Milch, milch, the milk;
der Wein, vine, the wine;
das Bier, beer, the beer;
das Frühstück, frü'-stück, the breakfast;
das Mittagessen, mit''-tâhchs-ess'-sen, the dinner;
das Vesperbrot, fes''-per-brote', the afternoon's luncheon;
das Abendessen, â''-bent-ess'-sen, the supper.

5. Kleidungsstücke (clothing).

Der Rock, rock, the coat;
das Kleid, klite, the gown;
der Mantel, mân'-tel, the cloak;
die Weste, vess'-tai, the waistcoat;
die Jacke, yâck'-kai, the jacket;
die Hose, ho'-zai, the pantaloons;
die Unterhose, öön''-ter-ho'-zai, the drawers;
der Schuh, shoo, the shoe;
der Strumpf, ströömpf, the stocking;
der Stiefel, stee'-fel, the boot;
der Pantoffel, pân-tof'-fel, the slipper;
das Hemd, hemt, the shirt, shift;
der Unterrock, öön''-ter-rock', the petticoat;
die Schürze, shürr'-tsai, the apron;

der Handschuh, hânt'-shoo, the glove;
der Ring, ring (rink), the ring;
das Taschentuch, tâsh''-shen-tooch', the handkerchief;
der Hut, hoot, the hat;
die Mütze, müt'-tsai, the cap;
die Uhr, oor, the watch;
der Regenschirm, rai''-ghen-shirrm', the umbrella;
der Sonnenschirm, zon''-nen-shirrm', the parasol;
der Fächer, fech'-cher, the fan;
der Stock, stock, the cane;
der Beutel, boi'-tel, the purse;
die Brille, bril'-lai, the spectacles.

7. Der menſchliche Körper (the human body).

Der Menſch, mensh, the man;
der Körper, körr'-per, the body;
der Kopf, kopf, the head;
das Haar, hâhr, the hair;
das Geſicht, gai-zicht', the face;
die Stirne, stirr'-nai, the forehead;
das Auge, ou'-gai, the eye;
die Naſe, nâ'-zai, the nose;
das Ohr, ore, the ear;
der Mund, möönt, the mouth;
das Kinn, kin, the chin;
der Bart, bâhrt, the beard;
die Lippe, lip'-pai, the lip ;
der Zahn, tsâhn, the tooth;
die Zunge, tsööng'-ai, the tongue;

der Hals, hâlss, the neck;
die Schulter, shööl'-ter, the shoulder;
der Rücken, rük'-ken, the back;
der Arm, ârrm, the arm ;
die Hand, hânt, the hand;
der Finger, fing'-er, the finger;
der Nagel, nâ'-ghel, the nail;
die Bruſt, brööst, the breast;
das Herz, herrts, the heart;
der Magen, mâ'-ghen, the stomach;
das Bein, bine, the leg;
der Fuß, fooss, the foot;
das Knie, k'nee (k pronounced), the knee;
die Zehe, tsey'-hai, the toe;
das Gehirn, gai-hirrn', the brain.

8. Vierfüßige Thiere (quadrupeds).

Das Thier, teer, the animal;
das Pferd, pfairrt, the horse;
der Eſel, ai'-zel, the donkey;
der Hund, höönt, the dog;
die Katze, kât'-tsai, the cat;
die Ratte, rat'-tai, the rat;
die Maus, mouse, the mouse;
der Maulwurf, moul'-vöörf, the mole;
das Schwein, shwine, the pig;
die Ziege, tsee'-gai, the goat;
die Gemſe, ghem'-zai, the chamois;
der Haſe, hâ'-zai, the hare,
das Eichhorn, i'ch'-horn, the squirrel;
der Affe, âf'-fai, the monkey;

der Hirſch, hirrsh, the stag;
das Reh, rey, the roe;
der Ochſe, ock'-sai, the ox;
der Stier, steer, the bull;
die Kuh, koo, the cow;
das Kalb, kâlp, the calf;
das Schaf, shâhf, the sheep;
das Lamm, lâm, the lamb;
der Fuchs, fööcks, the fox;
der Wolf, völf, the wolf;
der Bär, bair, the bear ;
der Löwe, lö'-vai, the lion;
das Kameel, câm-meyl', the camel;
der Elephant, ai-lai-fânt', the elephant.

9. Vögel (birds).

Der Vogel, fo'-ghel, the bird;
der Hahn, hâhn, the cock;
das Huhn, hoon, the hen;
das Hühnchen, hü'n'-chen, the chicken;
der Schwan, shwâhn, the swan;
die Gans, gânss, the goose;
die Ente, en'-tai, the duck;
die Taube, tou'-bai, the pigeon;
der Pfau, pfou, the peacock;
die Wachtel, vâch'-tel, the quail;
die Schnepfe, shnep'-fai, the snipe;

das Rebhuhn, rep'-hoon, the partridge ;
der Krammetsvogel, krâm''-mets-fo'-ghel, the field-fare;
die Amſel, âm'-zel, the black-bird;
die Lerche, lerr'-chai, the lark;
die Nachtigall, nâch''-tee-gâl', the nightin-gale;
die Schwalbe, shwâl'-bai, the swallow·
der Zeiſig, tsi'-zich, the green-finch;
der Fink, fink, the finch;
der Sperling, sperr'-link, the sparrow

10. Fiſche, Inſekten ꝛc. (fishes, insects, etc.)

Der Fiſch, fish, the fish;
der Hecht, hecht, the pike;
der Lachs, lâcks, the salmon ;
der Karpfen, kârrp'-fen, the carp;
die Schleie, shli'-ai, the tench,
der Aal, âhl, the eel;

die Forelle, fo-rel'-lai, the trout;
die Kröte, krö'-tai, the toad;
der Froſch, frösh, the frog;
der Wurm, vöörm, the worm;
die Raupe, rou'-pai, the caterpillar·
die Ameiſe, â'-mi-zai, the ant;

die Spinne, spin'-nai, the spider;
die Laus, louse, the louse;
der Häring, hey'-rink, the herring;
die Auster, ou'-ster, the oyster;
die Muschel, mŏŏsh'-shel, the muscle-fish;
der Krebs, kraips, the craw-fish;

die Schlange, shlâng'-ai, the snake;
der Floh, flo, the flea;
die Fliege, flee'-gai, the fly;
die Biene, bee'-nai, the bee;
die Wespe, vess'-pai, the wasp;
der Schmetterling, shmet'-ter-link, the but-
[terfly.

11. Bäume und Blumen (trees and flowers).

Der Baum, boum, the tree;
der Apfelbaum, âp''-fel-boum', the apple-
tree;
der Birnbaum, birrn'-boum, the pear-tree;
der Pflaumenbaum, pflou''-men-boum',
the plum-tree;
der Kirschbaum, kirsh'-boum, the cherry-
tree;
der Nußbaum, nŏŏss'-boum, the nut-tree;
die Eiche, i'-chai, the oak-tree;
die Fichte, fich'-tai, the pine-tree;
die Tanne, tân'-nai, the fir-tree;
die Buche, boo'-chai, the beech;
die Ulme, ŏŏl'-mai, the elm;
die Pappel, pâp'-pel, the poplar;

die Blume, bloo'-mai, the flower;
die Rose, ro'-zai, the rose;
die Nelke, nel'-kai, the pink;
die Tulpe, tŏŏl'-pai, the tulip;
die Lilie, lee'-lee-ai, the lily;
die Levkoje, lef-ko'-yai, the gilliflower;
das Veilchen, file'-chen, the violet;
die Maiblume, mi''-bloo'-mai, the lily of
the valley;
die Kornblume, korrn''-bloo'-mai, the corn-
flower;
der Flieder, flee'-der, the elder;
die Sonnenblume, zon''-nen-bloo'-mai, the
sun-flower;
das Geisblatt, ghice'-blât, the honey-suckle.

12. Das Land (country).

Das Land, lânt, the country, land;
das Feld, felt, the field;
die Gegend, ghey'-ghent, the country;
die Ebene, ai'-bai-nai, the plain;
der Berg, berrch, the mountain;
das Thal, tâhl, the valley;
der Wald, vâlt, the forest;
der Busch, bŏŏsh, the copse;
der Weg, vaich, the road;
der Bach, bâch, the brook;
die Wiese, vee'-zai, the meadow;
die Haide, hi'-dai, the heath;
der Hügel, hü'-ghel, the hill;

die Hütte, hüt'-tai, the cottage;
das Dorf, dorrf, the village;
der Flecken, fleck'-ken, the borough;
das Schloß, shloss, the castle;
der Meierhof, mi''-er-ho'f', the farm;
die Mühle, müh'-lai, the mill;
das Korn, korrn, the corn;
der Weizen, vite'-sen, the wheat;
die Gerste, gherr'-stai, the barley;
der Hafer, hâ'-fer, the oats;
das Stroh, stro, the straw;
das Heu, hoi, the hay;
die Traube, trou'-bai, the bunch of grapes.

Leichte Gespräche. EASY DIALOGUES.

1.

Essen und Trinken. Eating and drinking.

Are you hungry?	Sind Sie hungrig?	Zint zee höŏng′-rich?
I have a good appetite.	Ich habe guten Appetit.	Ich hâ′-bai göŏ′-ten âp-pai-teet′.
I am very hungry.	Ich bin sehr hungrig.	Ich bin zeyr höŏng′-rich.
Eat something.	Essen Sie etwas.	Ess′-sen zee et′-vâss.
What will you eat?	Was wollen Sie essen?	Vâss vol′-len zee ess′-sen?
What do you wish to eat?	Was wünschen Sie zu essen?	Vâss vün′-shen zee tsoo ess′-sen?
You do not eat.	Sie essen nicht.	Zee ess′-sen nicht.
I beg your pardon; I eat very heartily.	Ich bitte um Verzeihung, ich esse sehr viel.	Ich bit′-tai öŏm ferr-tsi′-höŏnk, ich ess′-sai zeyr feel.
I have eaten very heartily.	Ich habe sehr viel gegessen.	Ich hâ′-bai zeyr feel gai-ghess′-sen.
I have dined with a good appetite.	Ich habe mit gutem Appetit zu Mittag gegessen.	Ich hâ′-bai mit goo′-tem âp-pai-teet′ tsoo mit-tâhch′ gai-ghess′-sen.
Eat another piece.	Essen Sie noch ein Stückchen.	Ess′-sen zee noch ine stück′-chen.
I can eat no more.	Ich kann nichts mehr essen.	Ich kân nichts meyr ess′-sen.
Are you thirsty?	Sind Sie durstig?	Zint zee döŏr′-stich?
Are you not thirsty?	Haben Sie keinen Durst?	Hâ′-ben zee keinen döŏrst.
I am very thirsty.	Ich bin sehr durstig.	Ich bin zeyr döŏr′-stich.
I am dying of thirst.	Ich vergehe vor Durst.	Ich fer-ghey′-hai fore döŏrst.
Let us drink.	Lassen Sie uns trinken.	Lâss′-sen zee öŏnss trink′-en.
Give me something to drink.	Geben Sie mir zu trinken.	Gai′-ben zee meer tsoo trink′-en.
Will you drink a glass of wine?	Wollen Sie ein Glas Wein trinken?	Vol′-len zee ine glâhss vine trink′-en?
Drink a glass of beer.	Trinken Sie ein Glas Bier.	Trink′-en zee ine glâhss beer
Drink another glass of wine.	Trinken Sie noch ein Glas Wein.	Trink′-en zee noch ine glâhss vine.
Sir, I drink to your health.	Mein Herr, ich trinke auf Ihre Gesundheit.	Mine herr, ich trink′-ai ouf ee′-rai gai-zöŏnt′-hite.
I have the honor, to drink to your health.	Ich habe die Ehre, auf Ihre Gesundheit zu trinken.	Ich hâ′-bai dee ey′-rai, ouf ee′-rai gai-zöŏnt′-hite tsoo trink′-en.

2.

Gehen und Kommen. Going and coming.

Where are you going?	Wohin gehen Sie?	Vo-hin′ ghey′-hen zee?
I am going home.	Ich gehe nach Hause.	Ich ghey′-hai nâch hou′-zai.
I was going to your house.	Ich wollte zu Ihnen.	Ich vol′-tai tsoo ee′-nen.
Where do you come from?	Woher kommen Sie.	Vo-hair′ kom′-men zee?

I come from my brother's.	Ich komme von meinem Bruder.	Ich kom'-mai fon mi'-nem broo'-der.
I am coming from church.	Ich komme aus der Kirche.	Ich kom'-mai ouss dair kirr'-chai.
I just left the school.	Ich komme so eben aus der Schule.	Ich kom'-mai zo ai'-ben ouss dair shoo'-lai.
Will you go with me?	Wollen Sie mit mir gehen?	Vol'-len zee mit meer ghey'-hen?
Whither do you wish to go?	Wohin wollen Sie gehen?	Vo'-hin vol'-len zee ghey'-hen?
We will go for a walk.	Wir wollen spazieren gehen.	Veer vol'-len spât-zee'-ren ghey'-hen.
We will take a walk.	Wir wollen einen Spaziergang machen.	Veer vol'-len i'-nen spât-seer'-gânk mâch'-chen.
With all my heart, most willingly.	Sehr gern, mit Vergnügen.	Zeyr gherrn, mit fer-g'nü'-ghen.
What way shall we take?	Welchen Weg wollen wir nehmen?	Vel'-chen vaich vol'-len veer nai'-men?
Any way you like.	Welchen Weg Sie wollen.	Vel'-chen vaich zee vol'-len.
Let us go into the park.	Lassen Sie uns in den Park gehen.	Lâss'-sen zee ööns in dain pârrk ghey'-hen.
Let us take your friend in our way.	Lassen Sie uns im Vorbeigehen Ihren Freund abholen.	Lâss'-sen zee ööns im fore-bi''-ghey'-hen ee'-ren froint âp''-ho'-len.
As you please.	Wie es Ihnen gefällig ist.	Vee ess ee'-nen gai-fel'-lich ist.
Is Mr. B. at home?	Ist Herr B. zu Hause?	Ist herr B. tsoo hou'-zai?
He is gone out.	Er ist ausgegangen.	Air ist ouss''-gai-gâng'-en.
He is not at home.	Er ist nicht zu Hause.	Air ist nicht tsoo hou'-zai.
Can you tell us, where he is gone?	Können Sie uns sagen, wohin er gegangen ist?	Kön'-nen zee ööns zâ'-ghen, vo-hin' air gai-gâng'-en ist?
I cannot tell you precisely.	Ich kann es Ihnen nicht gewiß sagen.	Ich kân ess ee'-nen nicht gai-viss' zâ'-ghen.
I think, he is gone to see his sister.	Ich glaube, daß er zu seiner Schwester gegangen ist.	Ich glou'-bai, dâss air tsoo zi'-ner shwes'-ter gai-gâng'-en ist.
Do you know, when he will come back?	Wissen Sie, wann er zurückkommt?	Viss'-sen zee, vân air tsoo-rück'-komt?
No, he said nothing of it, when he went out.	Nein; er hat nichts davon gesagt, als er ging.	Nine, air hâht nichts dâ-fon' gai-zâ'cht', âlss air ghink.
Then we must go without him.	Dann müssen wir ohne ihn gehen.	Dân müss'-sen veer oh'-nai een ghey'-hen.

8.
Fragen und Antworten. Questions and answers.

Come nearer; I have something to tell you.	Treten Sie näher, ich habe Ihnen etwas zu sagen.	Trai'-ten zee nai'-her, ich hâ'-bai ee'-nen et'-vâss tsoo zâ'-ghen.
I have a word to say to you.	Ich habe Ihnen ein Wörtchen zu sagen.	Ich hâ'-bai ee'-nen ine vörrt'-chen tsoo zâ'-ghen.
Listen to me.	Hören Sie mich an.	Hö'-ren zee mich ân.
I want to speak to you.	Ich möchte mit Ihnen sprechen.	Ich möch'-tai mit ee'-nen sprech'-chen.
What is your pleasure?	Was steht zu Ihren Diensten?	Vâss steyt tsoo ee'-ren deen'-sten?
I am speaking to you.	Ich spreche mit Ihnen.	Ich sprech'-chai mit ee'-nen.

English	German	Pronunciation
I am not speaking to you.	Ich spreche nicht mit Ihnen.	Ich sprech'-chai nicht mit ee'-nen.
What do you say?	Was sagen Sie?	Vâss zâ'-ghen zee?
What did you say?	Was haben Sie gesagt?	Vâss hâ'-ben zee gai-zâ'cht'?
I say nothing.	Ich sage nichts.	Ich zâ'-gai nichts.
Do you hear?	Hören Sie?	Hö'-ren zee?
Do you hear what I say?	Verstehen Sie, was ich sage?	Fer-stai'-hen zee, vâss ich zâ'-gai?
Do you understand me?	Verstehen Sie mich?	Fer-stai'-hen zee mich?
Will you be so kind, as to repeat....?	Wollen Sie so gut sein, zu wiederholen....?	Vol'-len zee zo goot zine, tsoo vee'-der-ho''-len....?
I understand you well.	Ich verstehe Sie wohl.	Ich fer-stai'-hai zee vole.
Why do you not answer me?	Warum antworten Sie mir nicht?	Vâ'-röom ânt''-vorr'-ten zee meer nicht?
Do you not speak French?	Sprechen Sie nicht Französisch?	Sprech'-chen zee nicht frân-tsö'-zish?
Very little, Sir.	Sehr wenig, mein Herr.	Seyr vai'-nich, mine herr.
I understand it a little, but I do not speak it.	Ich verstehe es ein wenig, aber ich spreche es nicht.	Ich fer-stey'-hai ess ine vai'-nich, â'-ber ich sprech'-chai ess nicht.
Speak louder.	Sprechen Sie lauter.	Sprech'-chen zee lou'-ter.
Do not speak so loud.	Sprechen Sie nicht so laut.	Sprech'-chen zee nicht zo lout.
Do not make so much noise.	Machen Sie nicht so viel Lärm.	Mâch'-chen zee nicht zo feel lerrm.
Hold your tongue.	Schweigen Sie.	Shwi'-ghen zee.
Did you not tell me, that....?	Sagten Sie mir nicht, daß....?	Zâhch'-ten zee meer nicht, dâss....?
Who told you that?	Wer hat Ihnen das gesagt?	Vair hâht ee'-nen dâss gai-zâhcht'?
They have told me so.	Man hat es mir gesagt.	Mân hâht ess meer gai-zâhcht'.
Somebody has told me so.	Es hat mir's Jemand gesagt.	Ess hâht meer'ss yai'-mânt gai-zâhcht.
I have heard it.	Ich habe es gehört.	Ich hâ'-bai ess gai-hö'rt.
What do you wish to say?	Was wollen Sie sagen?	Vâss vol'-len zee zâ'-ghen?
What is that good for?	Wozu soll das dienen?	Vo-tsoo' sol dâss dee'-nen?
How do you call that?	Wie nennen Sie das?	Vee nen'-nen zee dâss?
That is called....	Das heißt....	Dâss hi'sst....
May I ask you....?	Darf ich Sie fragen....?	Dârf ich zee frâ'-ghen....?
What do you wish?	Was wünschen Sie?	Vâss vün'-shen zee?
Do you know Mr. G.?	Kennen Sie Herrn G.?	Ken'-nen zee herrn G.?
I know him by sight.	Ich kenne ihn von Ansehen.	Ich ken'-nai een fon ân''-zey'-hen.
I know him by name.	Ich kenne ihn dem Namen nach.	Ich ken'-nai een dem nâ'-men nâch.

4.

Das Alter. The age.

English	German	Pronunciation
How old are you?	Wie alt sind Sie?	Vee âlt zint zee?
How old is your brother?	Wie alt ist Ihr Herr Bruder?	Vee âlt ist eer herr broo'-der?
I am twelve years old.	Ich bin zwölf Jahre alt.	Ich bin tswölf yâ'-rai âlt.
I am ten years and six months old.	Ich bin zehn und ein halbes Jahr alt.	Ich bin tsain öönt ine hâl'-bess yâhr âlt.
Next month I shall be sixteen years old.	Im nächsten Monat werde ich sechzehn Jahre alt.	Im naich'-sten mo'-nât verr'-dai ich zech'-tsain yâ'-rai âlt.

I was eighteen years old last week.	Vergangene Woche bin ich achtzehn Jahre alt geworben.	Fer-gång'-ai-nai voch'-chai bin ich åcht'-tsain yå'-rai ålt gai-vorr'-den.
You do not look so old.	Sie sehen nicht so alt aus.	Zee zey'-hen nicht zo ålt ouss.
You look older.	Sie sehen älter aus.	Zee zey'-hen el'-ter ouss.
I thought, you were older.	Ich hielt Sie für älter.	Ich heelt zee für el'-ter.
I did not think you were so old.	Ich hielt Sie nicht für so alt.	Ich heelt zee nicht für zo ålt.
How old may your uncle be?	Wie alt mag Ihr Oheim sein?	Vee ålt må'ch eer o'-hime zine?
He may be sixty years old.	Er kann etwa sechzig Jahre haben.	Air kån et'-vå zech'-tsich yå'-rai hå'-ben.
He is about sixty years old.	Er ist ungefähr sechzig Jahre alt.	Air ist öön''-gai-fair' zech'-tsich yåh'-rai ålt.
He is more than fifty years old.	Er ist über fünfzig Jahre alt.	Air ist ü'-ber fünf'-tsich yåh'-rai ålt.
He is a man of fifty and upwards.	Er ist ein Mann von fünfzig und einigen Jahren.	Air ist ine mån fon fünf'-tsich öönt i'-nig-en yå'-ren.
He may be sixty or there abouts.	Er kann etwa sechzig Jahre zählen.	Air kån et'-vå zech'-tsich yå'-rai tsai'-len.
He is above eighty.	Er ist über achtzig Jahre.	Air ist ü'-ber åcht'-tsich yå'-rai.
That is a great age.	Das ist ein hohes Alter.	Dåss ist ine ho'-hess ål'-ter
Is he so old?	Ist er so alt?	Ist air zo ålt?
He begins to grow old.	Er fängt an zu altern.	Air fenkt ån tsoo ål'-tern.

5.
Die Zeit. The time.

What o'clock is it?	Wie viel Uhr ist es?	Vee feel oor ist ess?
Pray tell me what time it is.	Ich bitte, sagen Sie mir, welche Zeit es ist.	Ich bit'-tai, zå'-ghen zee meer, vel'-chai tsite ess ist.
It is one o'clock.	Es ist ein Uhr.	Ess ist ine oor.
It is past one.	Es ist ein Uhr vorbei.	Ess ist ine oor fore-bi'.
It has struck one.	Es hat eins geschlagen.	Ess håht i'nss gai-shlå'-ghen.
It is a quarter past one.	Es ist ein Viertel auf zwei.	Ess ist ine feer'-tel ouf tsvi.
It is half past one.	Es ist halb zwei.	Ess ist hålp tsvi.
It wants ten minutes of two.	Es fehlen zehn Minuten an zwei.	Ess fai'-len tsain mee-noo'-ten ån tsvi.
It is not yet two o'clock.	Es ist noch nicht zwei Uhr.	Ess ist noch nicht tsvi oor.
It is only twelve o'clock.	Es ist erst zwölf.	Ess ist eyrst tsvölf.
It is almost three o'clock.	Es ist beinahe drei.	Ess ist bi-nå'-hai dri.
It is on the stroke of three.	Es ist gegen drei.	Ess ist ghey'-ghen dri.
It is going to strike three.	Es wird gleich drei Uhr schlagen.	Ess virrt gli'ch dri oor shlå' ghen.
It is ten minutes past three.	Es ist zehn Minuten nach drei.	Ess ist tsain mee-noo'-ten nåch dri.
The clock is going to strike.	Die Uhr wird sogleich schlagen.	Dee oor virrt zo-gli'ch' shlå'-ghen.
There the clock strikes.	Da schlägt die Uhr.	Då shlai'cht dee oor.
It is not late.	Es ist nicht spät.	Ess ist nicht spait.
It is later than I thought.	Es ist später, als ich dachte.	Ess ist spai'-ter, ålss ich dåch'-tai.
I did not think it was so late.	Ich dachte nicht, daß es so spät wäre.	Ich dåch'-tai nicht, dåss ess zo spait vai'-rai.

5*

6.

Das Wetter. The weather.

What kind of weather is it?	Was ist es für Wetter?	Vâss ist ess fü'r vet'-ter?
It is bad weather.	Es ist schlechtes Wetter.	Ess ist shlech'-tess vet'-ter.
It is very cloudy.	Es ist trübe.	Ess ist trü'-bai.
It is dreadful weather.	Es ist ein abscheuliches Wetter.	Ess ist ine âp-shoi'-lich-chess vet'-ter.
It is fine weather.	Es ist schönes Wetter.	Ess ist shö'-ness vet'-ter.
We are going to have a fine day.	Wir werden einen schönen Tag haben.	Veer verr'-den i'-nen shö'-nen tâhch hâ'-ben.
It is dewy.	Der Thau fällt.	Dair tou fellt.
It is foggy.	Es ist neblig.	Ess ist nai'-bai-lich.
It is rainy weather.	Es ist regnerisches Wetter.	Ess ist raich'-nai-rish-shess vet'-ter.
It threatens to rain.	Es droht zu regnen.	Ess dro't tsoo raich'-nen.
The sky becomes very cloudy.	Der Himmel umzieht sich.	Dair him'-mel ŏŏm-tseet' zich.
The sky is getting very dark.	Der Himmel wird dunkel.	Dair him'-mel virrt dŏŏnk'-el.
The sun is coming out.	Die Sonne fängt an sich zu zeigen.	Dee zon'-nai fenkt ân zich tsoo tsi'-ghen.
The weather is clearing up again.	Das Wetter klärt sich wieder auf.	Dâss vet'-ter klairt zich vee'-der ouf.
It is very hot.	Es ist sehr heiß.	Ess ist zeyr hice.
It is sultry.	Es ist eine erstickende Hitze.	Es ist i'-nai err-stick'-ken-dai hit'-sai.
It is very mild.	Es ist sehr mild.	Ess ist zeyr mīlt.
It is cold.	Es ist kalt.	Ess ist kâlt.
It is excessively cold.	Es ist eine übermäßige Kälte.	Ess ist i'-nai ü''-ber-mai'-sig-ai kel'-tai.
It is raw weather.	Es ist rauhes Wetter.	Ess ist rou'-hess vet'-ter.
It rains.	Es regnet.	Ess raich'-net.
It has been raining.	Es hat geregnet.	Ess hâht gai-raich'-net.
It is going to rain.	Es wird gleich regnen.	Ess virrt gli'ch raich'-nen.
I feel some drops of rain.	Ich fühle Regentropfen.	Ich fü'-lai rai''-ghen-trop'-fen.
There are some drops of rain falling.	Es fallen Regentropfen.	Ess fâl'-len rai''-ghen-trop'-fen.
It hails.	Es hagelt.	Ess hâ'-ghelt.
It snows; it is snowing.	Es schneit; es fällt Schnee.	Ess shnite; ess felt shney.
It has been snowing.	Es hat geschneit; es ist Schnee gefallen.	Ess hâht gai-shnite'; ess ist shney gai-fâl'-len.
It snows in large flakes.	Es schneit in großen Flocken.	Ess shnite in gro'-sen flock'-ken.
It freezes.	Es friert.	Ess freert.
It has frozen.	Es hat gefroren.	Ess hâht gai-fro'-ren.
It begins to get milder.	Es fängt an, gelinder zu werden.	Ess fenkt ân gai-lin'-der tsoo verr'-den.
It thaws.	Es thauet auf.	Ess tou'-et ouf.
It is very windy.	Es ist sehr windig.	Ess ist zeyr vin'-dich.
The wind is very high.	Der Wind weht stark.	Dair vīnt vait stârk.
There is no air stirring.	Es weht kein Lüftchen.	Ess vait kine lüft'-chen.
It lightens.	Es blitzt.	Ess blitst.

It has lightened all night.	Es hat die ganze Nacht geblitzt.	Ess häht dee gân'-tsai nâcht gai-blitst.
It thunders.	Es donnert.	Ess don'-nert.
The thunder roars.	Der Donner rollt.	Dair don'-ner rölt.
The lightning has struck.	Es hat eingeschlagen.	Ess häht ine''-gai-shlä'-ghen.
It is stormy weather.	Es ist stürmisches Wetter.	Ess ist stür'-mish-shess vet'-ter.
We shall have a thunderstorm.	Wir werden ein Gewitter bekommen.	Veer verr'-den ine gai-vit'-ter bai-kom'-men.
The sky begins to clear up.	Der Himmel fängt an, sich aufzuheitern.	Dair him'-mel fenkt ân, zich ouf''-tsoo-hi'-tern.
The weather is very unsettled.	Das Wetter ist sehr unbeständig.	Dâss vet'-ter ist zeyr oon''-bai-sten'-dich.
It is very muddy.	Es ist sehr schmutzig.	Ess ist zeyr shmööt'-sich.
It is very dusty.	Es ist sehr staubig.	Ess ist zeyr stou'-bich.
It is very slippery.	Es ist sehr glatt.	Ess ist zeyr glât.
It is bad walking.	Es ist schlechtes Gehen.	Ess ist shlech'-tess gey'-hen.
It is day-light.	Es ist Tag.	Ess ist tâhch.
It is dark.	Es ist dunkel.	Ess ist döönk'-el.
It is night.	Es ist Nacht.	Ess ist nâcht.
It is moon-light.	Der Mond scheint.	Dair mo'nt shi'nt.
Do you think it will be fine weather?	Glauben Sie, daß es gutes Wetter geben wird?	Glou'-ben zee, dâss ess goo'-tess vet'-ter gai'-ben virrt?
I do not think that it will rain.	Ich glaube nicht, daß es regnen wird.	Ich glou'-bai nicht, dâss ess raich'-nen virrt.
I am afraid it will rain.	Ich fürchte, es wird regnen.	Ich fürch'-tai, ess virrt raich'-nen.
I fear so.	Ich fürchte es.	Ich fürch'-tai ess.

7.

Der Gruß.　The salutation.

Good morning, Sir!	Guten Morgen, mein Herr!	Goo'-ten morr'-ghen, mine herr!
I wish you a good morning.	Ich wünsche Ihnen guten Morgen.	Ich vün'-shai ee'-nen goo'-ten morr'-ghen.
How do you do?	Wie befinden Sie sich?	Vee bai-fin'-den zee zich?
How is your health?	Wie geht es mit Ihrer Gesundheit?	Vee gheyt ess mit ee'-rer gai-zöönt'-hite?
Do you continue in good health?	Befinden Sie sich immer wohl?	Bai-fin'-den zee zich im'-mer vole?
Pretty good; and how is yours?	Ziemlich wohl, und Sie?	Tseem'-lich vole, öönt zee?
Are you well?	Sind Sie wohl?	Zint zee vole?
Very well, and you?	Sehr wohl, und Sie auch?	Zeyr vole, öönd zee ouch?
I am perfectly well.	Ich befinde mich sehr wohl.	Ich bai-fin'-dai mich zeyr vole.
And how is it with you?	Und wie geht es mit Ihnen?	öönt vee gheyt ess mit ee'-nen?
As usual.	Wie gewöhnlich.	Vee gai-vö'n'-lich.
Pretty well, thank God.	Ziemlich gut, Gott sei Dank.	Tseem'-lich goot, Got zi dânk.
I am very happy to see you well	Es freut mich sehr, Sie wohl zu sehen.	Ess froit mich zeyr, zee vole tsoo zey'-hen.

8.

Der Besuch. The visit.

English	German	Pronunciation
There is a knock.	Es klopft.	Ess klopft.
Somebody knocks.	Es klopft Jemand.	Ess klopft yai'-mânt.
Go and see who it is.	Geh' hin und sieh, wer da ist.	Ghey hin öönt zee, vair dâ ist.
Go and open the door.	Geh' und öffne die Thür.	Ghey öönt öf'-nai dee tü'r.
It is Mrs. B.	Es ist Madame B.	Ess ist mâ-dâm' B.
I wish you a good morning.	Ich wünsche Ihnen guten Morgen.	Ich vün'-shai ee'-nen goo'-ten morr'-ghen.
I am happy to see you.	Es freut mich, Sie zu sehen.	Ess froit mich, zee tsoo zey'-hen.
I have not seen you this age.	Es ist ein Jahrhundert, seit ich Sie nicht sah.	Ess ist ine yâhr-höön'-dert, zite ich zee nicht zâh.
It is a novelty to see you.	Es ist eine Seltenheit, Sie zu sehen.	Ess ist i'-nai zel'-ten-hite, zee tsoo zey'-hen.
Pray, sit down.	Setzen Sie sich, ich bitte.	Zet'-sen zee zich, ich bit'-tai.
Sit down, if you please.	Setzen Sie sich gefälligst.	Zet'-sen zee zich gai-fel'-lichst.
Take a seat.	Nehmen Sie Platz.	Nai'-men zee plâts.
Give a chair to the lady.	Gib Madame einen Stuhl.	Gheep mâ-dâm' i'-nen stool.
Will you stay and take some dinner with us?	Wollen Sie zum Mittagsessen bei uns bleiben.	Vol'-len zee tsööm mit''-tâhchss-ess'-sen by ööns bli'-ben?
I cannot stay.	Ich kann nicht bleiben.	Ich kân nicht bli'-ben.
I only came in to see how you are.	Ich bin nur gekommen, um zu erfahren, wie Sie sich befinden.	Ich bin nöör gai-kom'-men, ööm tsoo er-fâ'-ren, vee zee zich bai-fin'-den.
I must go.	Ich muß gehen.	Ich mööss ghey'-hen.
You are in a great hurry.	Sie sind sehr eilig.	Zee zint zeyr i'-lich.
Why are you in such a hurry?	Weshalb sind Sie so eilig?	Vess'-hâlp zint zee zo i'-lich?
I have a great many things to do.	Ich habe viel zu thun.	Ich hâ'-bai feel tsoo toon.
Surely you can stay a little longer.	Sie können wohl noch einen Augenblick bleiben.	Zee kön'-nen vole noch i'-nen ou''-ghen-blick' bli'-ben.
I will stay longer another time.	Ein ander Mal will ich länger bleiben.	Ine ân'-der mâhl vill ich leng'-er bli'-ben.
I thank you for your visit.	Ich danke Ihnen für Ihren Besuch.	Ich dânk'-ai ee'-nen für ee'-ren bai-zooch'.
I hope to see you soon again.	Ich hoffe Sie bald wieder zu sehen.	Ich hof'-fai zee bâlt vee'-der tsoo zey'-hen.

9.

Frühstück. Breakfast.

English	German	Pronunciation
Have you breakfasted?	Haben Sie gefrühstückt?	Hâ'-ben zee gai-frü'-stückt?
Not yet.	Noch nicht.	Noch nicht.
You are come just in time.	Sie kommen gerade zu rechter Zeit.	Zee kom'-men gai-râ'-dai tsoo rech'-ter tsite.
You will breakfast with us.	Sie werden mit uns frühstücken.	Zee verr'-den mit ööns früh'-stük'-ken.
Breakfast is ready.	Das Frühstück ist bereit.	Dâss frü'-stück ist bai-rite'.
Do you drink tea or coffee?	Trinken Sie Thee oder Kaffee?	Trink'-en zee tey o'-der kâf'-fai?

Would you prefer chocolate?	Wollen Sie vielleicht lieber Chocolade?	Vol'-len zee feel-li'cht' lee'-ber sho-ko-lâ'-dai.
I prefer coffee.	Ich ziehe den Kaffee vor.	Ich tsee'-hai dain kâf'-fai fore.
What can I offer you?	Was kann ich Ihnen anbieten?	Vâss kân ich ee'-nen ân''-bee'-ten?
Here are rolls and toast.	Hier sind Milchbrötchen und geröstetes Brot.	Here zint milch''-brö't'-chen öönt gai-röss'-tai-tess brote.
What do you like best?	Was mögen Sie am liebsten?	Vâss mö'-ghen zee âm leep'-sten?
I shall take a roll.	Ich werde ein Brötchen nehmen.	Ich verr'-dai ine brö't'-chen nai'-men.
How do you like the coffee?	Wie finden Sie den Kaffee?	Vee fin'-den zee dain kâf'-fai?
Is the coffee strong enough?	Ist der Kaffee stark genug?	Ist dair kâf'-fai stârrk gai-nooch'.
It is excellent.	Er ist vortrefflich.	Air ist fore-tref'-lich.
Is there enough sugar in it?	Ist genug Zucker darin?	Ist gai-nooch' tsöök'-ker dâ-rin'?
If there is not, do not make any ceremony.	Ist es nicht, so machen Sie keine Komplimente.	Ist ess nicht, zo mâch'-chen zee ki'-nai com-plee-men'-tai.
Do as if you were at home.	Thun Sie, als ob Sie zu Hause wären.	Toon zee, âlss op zee tsoo hou'-zai vai'-ren.

10.

Vor dem Mittagsessen. Before dinner.

At what time do we dine to-day?	Um welche Zeit essen wir heute zu Mittag?	öm vel'-chai tsite ess'-sen veer hoi'-tai tsoo mit'-tâhch?
We shall dine at two o'clock.	Wir werden um zwei Uhr essen.	Veer verr'-den öm tsvi oor ess'-sen.
We shall not dine before three o'clock.	Wir werden nicht vor drei Uhr essen.	Veer verr'-den nicht fore dri oor ess'-sen.
Shall we have anybody at dinner to-day?	Werden wir heute zum Essen Jemanden bei uns haben?	Verr'-den veer hoi'-tai tsöm ess'-sen yai'-mân-den by öönss hâ'-ben?
Do you expect company?	Erwarten Sie Gesellschaft?	Er-vârr'-ten zee gai-zel'-shâft?
I expect Mr. B.	Ich erwarte Herrn B.	Ich er-vârr'-tai herrn B.
Mr. D. has promised to come if the weather permits it.	Herr D. hat versprochen zu kommen, wenn es das Wetter erlaubt.	Herr D. hâht fer-sproch'-chen, tsoo kom'-men, ven ess dâss vet'-ter er-loupt'.
Have you given orders for dinner?	Haben Sie die Befehle zum Mittagsessen gegeben?	Hâ'-ben zee dee bai-fai'-lai tsöm mit''-tâhchss-ess'-sen gai-gai'-ben?
What have you ordered for dinner?	Was haben Sie zum Essen bestellt?	Vâss hâ'-ben zee tsöm ess'-sen bai-stellt'?
Have you sent for fish?	Haben Sie Fisch besorgen lassen?	Hâ'-ben zee fish bai-zorr'-ghen lâss'-sen?
I could not get any fish.	Ich habe keinen Fisch bekommen können.	Ich hâ'-bai ki'-nen fish bai-kom'-men kön'-nen.
I fear, we shall have a very indifferent dinner.	Ich besorge, daß wir kein sonderliches Mittagsessen haben werden.	Ich bai-zorr'-gai, dâss veer kine zon'-der-lich-ches mit''-tâhchss-ess'-sen hâ'-ben verr'-den.
We must do as we can.	Wir müssen uns behelfen.	Veer müss'-sen öönss bai-hel'-fen.

11.

Mittagsessen. Dinner.

English	German	Pronunciation
What shall I help you to?	Was soll ich Ihnen vorlegen?	Vâss zol ich ee'-nen fore''-lai'-ghen?
Will you take a little soup?	Wollen Sie etwas Suppe?	Vol'-len zee et'-vâss zööp'-pai?
No, I thank you. I will trouble you for a little beef.	Ich danke. Ich werde Sie um etwas Rindfleisch bitten.	Ich dânk'-ai. Ich verr'-dai zee ŏŏm et'-vâss rint'-flii'sh bit'-ten.
It looks so very nice.	Es sieht so gut aus.	Ess zeet zo goot ouss.
Which piece do you like best?	Welches Stück haben Sie am liebsten?	Vel'-ches stück hâ'-ben zee am leep'-sten.
I hope this piece is to your liking.	Ich hoffe, daß dies Stück nach Ihrem Geschmacke ist.	Ich hof'-fai, dâss deess stück nâch ee'-rem gai-shmâck'-kai ist.
Gentlemen, you have the dishes near you.	Meine Herren, die Schüsseln stehen vor Ihnen.	Mi'-nai herr'-ren, dee shüss'-seln stai'-hen fore ee'-nen.
Help yourselves.	Bedienen Sie sich.	Bai-dee'-nen zee zich.
Take without ceremony what you like best.	Nehmen Sie ohne Umstände, was Ihnen beliebt.	Nai'-men zee oh'-nai ŏŏm'-sten-dai, vâss ee'-nen bai-leept'.
Would you like a little of this roast-meat?	Wollen Sie ein wenig von diesem Braten?	Vol'-len zee ine vey'-nich fon dee'-zem brâ'-ten?
Do you choose some fat?	Wollen Sie Fettes?	Vol'-len zee fet'-tess?
Give me some of this lean, if you please.	Geben Sie mir Mageres, wenn es Ihnen gefällig ist.	Gai'-ben zee meer mâ'-gai-ress, ven ess ee'-nen gai-fel'-lich ist.
How do you like the roast-meat?	Wie finden Sie den Braten?	Vee fin'-den zee dain brâ'-ten?
It is excellent, delicious.	Er ist vortrefflich, köstlich.	Air ist fore-tref'-lich, köst'-lich.
What will you take with your meat?	Was wünschen Sie zum Fleisch?	Vâss vün'-shen zee tsŏŏm flii'sh?
May I help you to some vegetables?	Darf ich Ihnen Gemüse geben?	Dârf ich ee'-nen gai-mü'-zai gai'-ben.
Will you take peas or cauliflower?	Wünschen Sie Erbsen oder Blumenkohl?	Vün'-shen zee errp'-zen o'-der bloo''-men-kole'?
It is quite indifferent to me.	Es ist mir ganz gleich.	Ess ist meer gânts gli'ch.
I shall send you a piece of this fowl.	Ich will Ihnen ein Stückchen von diesem Geflügel reichen.	Ich vil ee'-nen ine stück'-chen fon dee'-zem gai-flü'-ghel ri'-chen.
No, thank you, I can eat no more.	Ich danke, ich kann nichts mehr essen.	Ich dânk'-ai, ich kân nichts meyr ess'-sen.
You are a poor eater.	Sie sind ein schwacher Esser.	Zee zint ine shwâch'-cher ess'-ser.
You eat nothing.	Sie essen gar nichts.	Zee ess'-sen gâhr nichts.
I beg your pardon, I do honor to your dinner.	Ich bitte um Verzeihung, ich mache Ihrem Essen Ehre.	Ich bit'-tai ŏŏm fer-tsi'-hŏŏnk, ich mâch'-chai ee'-rem ess'-sen ey'-rai.
You may take away.	Ihr könnt nun abdecken.	Eer könt nŏŏn âp''-deck'-ken.

12.

Thee. Tea.

English	German	Pronunciation
Have you carried in the tea-things?	Hast du Alles gebracht, was zum Thee gehört?	Hâhst doo âl'-les gai-brâcht', vâss tsŏŏm tey gai-hö'rt'?
Everything is on the table.	Es ist Alles auf dem Tische.	Ess ist âl'-less ouf dem tish'-shai

Does the water boil?	Kocht das Wasser?	Kocht dâss vâss'-ser?
Tea is ready?	Der Thee ist fertig.	Dair tey ist ferr'-tich.
They are waiting for you.	Sie werden erwartet.	Zee verr'-den er-wârr'-tet.
Here I am.	Hier bin ich.	Here bin ich.
We have not cups enough.	Wir haben nicht Tassen genug.	Veer hâ'-ben nicht tâss'-sen gai-nooch'.
We want two more cups and saucers.	Wir müssen noch zwei Tassen haben.	Veer müss'-sen noch tsvi tâss'-sen hâ'-ben.
Bring another tea-spoon and a saucer.	Bringe noch einen Theelöffel und eine Untertasse.	Bring'-ai noch i'-nen tey''-löff'-fel öönt i'-nai öön''-ter-tâss'-sai.
You have not brought in the sugar-tongs.	Du hast die Zuckerzange nicht gebracht.	Doo hâhst dee tsööck''-kertsäng'-ai nicht gai-brâcht'
Do you take cream?	Nehmen Sie Rahm?	Nai'-men zee râhm?
The tea is so strong.	Der Thee ist so stark.	Dair tey ist zo stârk.
I shall thank you for a little more milk.	Ich werbe noch um etwas Milch bitten.	Ich verr'-dai noch öm et'-vâss milch bit'-ten.
Here are cakes and muffins.	Hier ist Kuchen und Brotkuchen.	Here ist koo'-chen öönt brote''-koo'-chen.
Do you prefer some bread and butter?	Essen Sie lieber Butterbrot?	Ess'-sen zee lee'-ber bööt''-ter-brote'?
I shall take a slice of bread and butter.	Ich werbe ein Butterbrot nehmen.	Ich verr'-dai ine bööt''-ter-brote' nai'-men.
Pass the plate this way.	Schieb' den Teller hierher.	Sheep dain tel'-ler here'-hair.
Ring the bell, if you please.	Schellen Sie gefälligst.	Shel'-len zee gai-fel'-lichst.
Will you kindly ring the bell?	Wollen Sie gütigst die Klingel ziehen?	Vol'-len zee gü'-tichst dee kling'-el tsee'-hen?
We want some more water.	Wir brauchen noch mehr Wasser.	Veer brou'-chen noch mair vâss'-ser.
Bring it as quickly as possible.	Bringe es so schnell als möglich.	Bring'-ai ess zo shnel âlss mö'ch'-lich.
Make haste.	Beeile dich.	Bai-i'-lai dich.
Take the plate with you.	Nimm den Teller mit.	Nim dain tel'-ler mit.
Is your tea sweet enough?	Ist der Thee süß genug?	Ist dair tey zü'ss gai-nooch'.
Have I put sugar enough in your tea?	Habe ich genoug' Zucker in Ihren Thee gethan?	Hâ'-bai ich gai-nooch' tsööck''-ker in ee'-ren tey gai-tâhn'?
It is excellent.	Er ist vortrefflich.	Air ist fore-tref'-lich.
I do not like it quite so sweet.	Ich habe ihn nicht gern so süß.	Ich hâ'-bai een nicht gherrn zo zü'ss.
Your tea is very good.	Ihr Thee ist sehr gut.	Eer tey ist zeyr goot.
Where do you buy it?	Wo kaufen Sie ihn?	Vo kou'-fen zee een?
I buy it at	Ich kaufe ihn bei	Ich kou'-fai een by ....
Have you already done?	Sind Sie schon fertig?	Zint zee shone ferr'-tich?
You will take another cup?	Sie werden noch eine Tasse nehmen.	Zee verr'-den noch i'-nai tâss'-sai nai'-men.
I shall pour you out half a cup.	Ich werde Ihnen noch eine halbe Tasse einschenken.	Ich verr'-dai ee'-nen noch i'-nai hâl'-bai tâss'-sai ine''-shenk'-en.
You will not refuse me.	Sie werden es mir nicht abschlagen.	Zee verr'-den ess meer nicht âp''-shlâ'-ghen.
I have already drunk three cups, and I never drink more.	Ich habe schon drei Tassen getrunken, und mehr trinke ich nie.	Ich hâ'-bai shone dri tâss'-sen gai-tröönk'-en, öönt meyr trink'-ai ich nee.